The Anomaly

By

G L Gardner-Shaw

 New Generation Publishing

For...

"Mum"
Janet Gardner

(b.1952 - d.2008)

Who will always be missed
Xxx

Acknowledgements

I would like to say thank you to my family especially Ken, Dad, Annabel, Harriet and Adam, for putting up with being ignored and for having the belief in me when I didn't. Also 'Aunty Vic' for interpreting my appalling handwriting and the kind use of her far superior typing skills.

Prologue

In the later part of the twenty first century – war again broke out in Europe. Climate change that was a continuous threat throughout the early part of the century had now come to fruition. The ice cap melted and dismay and disruption was caused throughout the main economic powers of Europe. Chemical and biological, weapons were used; fear spread throughout the population. No one trusted the food prepared or grown by anyone else. Little did they know but it was already too late.

People started to hide in the surrounding countryside, cities were abandoned to the elements, after the large scale destruction.

Eventually the 30-year war came to an abrupt end, with the sudden realisation of the demise of the sexes. Genetics was the key: to determine the sex of a child, cloning and genetically modified food became the norm as crops became the new 'breakthroughs' in modern science.

The biological weapons had reached their zenith attacking the unsuspecting populous with a creation that would attack the mainstay of human existence, every family was attacked creating a new world order.

The prestige of power became a magnet for unwholesome people. The world had now changed irrevocably; Europe had become a powerful state but all was not as it seemed. Time passed by, the years flowed into decades and the uneasy truce became the norm and the destruction of the human species was not unwelcomed by all.

6

Part One

Maria

1

Dark gloom lay over the trees, the rainy season was due any day now. Moonlight penetrated through the leaves, with a dappled light on the woodland floor, illuminating the three figures standing near a freshly dug hole. Each was weary from their exertions. Their heads were hung low.

"Do you think it is deep enough?" Eva carefully picked up a shining metallic object by the wooden handle, which glinted in the moonlight, and proceeded to remove the clods of soil from the far edge of the hole. "Where did you find this old thing?" She looked down at it in amazement.

"In the old part of the house, we had it in there on display. Apparently, it's called a shovel," Maria smiled at her granddaughter.

"Well I never. A bit archaic, but it does the job fine..." Slowly and methodically, Eva dug the trench deeper and longer. The others watched in silence. Eva sat down exhausted, examining the blisters appearing on the palms of her soft hands; her protruding stomach hindering her movement with every dig she made.

Staring into the swirling fog gently rising from the sea, curling around the dark erect tree trunks standing to attention. The atmosphere was almost claustrophobic absently she rubbed her sore hands picking freshly dug earth from her nails. As if she was a robot, she heaved herself back up from the rock using the shovel as leverage. Tucking her long auburn hair behind her ears she gently started to put pressure onto her spade easing more of the compacted earth loose to the nearby pile.

Eva was becoming short of breath, gasping for every intake. Her back felt as if it were crushing slowly into her stomach.

"I think that will be enough." Maria instructed.

"How can you say that Grandmother? Anyone could find this here." Eva knew she sounded petulant. She looked at her blistered hands; the brown soil embedded into every indentation. Her shoulders were heavy.

Soon the weight on them would be lifted. No more secrets, she had to remind herself. She hauled her weight off the mound, her legs giving way under the unusual strain. Nearby was a moss-covered rock, where she sat to give her tiny frame relief from the immense pressure on her spine. The stillness penetrated her very soul. Putting her arms behind her, she tilted her head back, and her long blond hair brushed the rock.

Trying not to view the scene that was before her, Eva looked towards the sky. The clouds drifted over the moon, embodying the eerie silence. She hated being here. She wanted to return to the mainland. Even at night, the heat was unbearable. Soon it would be the rainy season and she would get some relief.

Why did he have to die now? She turned back to the scene before her. How could she be related to these two women? She didn't have their strength. She would never be like them. Her Grandmother was even now beautiful her blonde hair wound elegantly on her head although small in stature she exuded an elegance, which belied her height, despite the burdens she had endured during her life. Not a flicker of doubt crossed their faces. How did they cope? She felt the guilt rise inside her, but she also felt relief. All her life she had been warned about being different. Always not fitting in, but why? No one had told her.

Engulfed by her own self-pity she stared at the reason why three fully-grown women were out in the dark, digging a hole. However, it was not a hole, it was her father's grave – their special secret. Her earliest memories were of being told not to mention 'him' to anyone; not even the visits from her grandmother were allowed to be mentioned. 'Just an old family friend,' her life was based on secrets. She sat down on the wet mossy floor, alone, always excluded never quite knowing why. Always 'their' little secret – never hers.

She looked over to the 'hole'. Her grandmother was too old to help her, her mother too ill, (after so many years of hiding without medical help). Therefore, it was down to her.

"Are you ready to lift?" Faith asked her.

"I think I'll manage; now my breathing has calmed down – it's this heat." Faith looked at her daughter. There was so much of her father in her – she would never admit it of course. She had denied his existence for so long. Her attention turned to the job at hand.

A smile of reassurance appeared on Eva's face as she realized the hurt that her mother must be feeling to grieve over someone that she had spent her whole life with. Eva bent down and placed the leaden arms across the body. Slowly she shifted her weight, putting her hands under the shoulders, digging her fingers into the aluminium blanket, enough to feel the soft flesh sink into the bones as she applied pressure. She was ready now. She checked her position carefully, balanced against her own weight and that of the child she was carrying. The wood around her enveloped her, pressing down on her mood. If she didn't know better, the trees were bending towards her. Nowhere was safe from prying eyes. Don't be stupid she kept telling herself. The pressure was getting to her and she was not strong enough mentally for this. A low guttural wail pierced into the oppressive silence surrounding them.

"Mum?" Eva whispered into the still cloying air, she

starred at her mother; panic was gripping her body, her insides stiffening her muscles as if she were paralysed.

Faith was bent in two, gripping so tightly onto the now stiffening body's ankles; her knuckles were white, almost luminescent in the night air. Tears gently rolled down her face to her chin. No other emotion was visible, except for the moisture on her cheeks. Eva stood, still gripping onto the bony flesh, not knowing what to do or how she was supposed to react. Maria, seeing her granddaughter's panic-stricken face, went over to comfort Faith, the woman who had kept her secret for the last twenty-five years.

"Say Goodbye. He will always be grateful to you for giving him a life – something he never thought he could have had. I also don't think I've ever said thank you, either." Maria put her arms around Faith, gently she patted her back letting the now crippled, sobbing Faith, rid herself of the pent up emotions of anger, guilt and responsibility.

Eva's fingers relaxed slowly, one by one, as she let the weight drop to the ground. She stood with the body at her feet, not daring to move, feeling the outsider as always. Her own inadequacies were always at the forefront of her mind. Coping with this baby was enough to make her feel queasy. If it had not been for the computer's bloody recommendation of age regulations, she would still be enjoying her carefree life.

"Why?" She shouted the word. Her mother and grandmother stopped consoling each other and stared at Eva in disbelief.

"Will you be quiet – you never know who may hear. Isn't that obvious, young lady?" Faith snapped. Her mother snapped out of her reverie and reverted to her normal severity.

"No, I will not shut up. I've always just kept my

mouth shut – to end up like this!" Eva swung her arms out towards her father's body and grave, not a metre away. "You have never told me why, do you know that – never! I have been made to feel unclean, unworthy, different, and never normal. Why?" Maria tried to regain her composure, breathing slowly.

"Why?" Eva's Grandmother turned on her, her face contorted into a venomous sneer, which terrified Eva, who had never seen her Grandmother react like this before. "You may ask what you want – now." Maria said, then pointing at Phillip. "That, is my son and your father, he deserved a life. It was not his mistake; nor your mother's, not even yours, but mine!" Eva was breathing deeply and trying not to lose the battle with the ever promise of tears, she looked at her Grandmother, stunned, unable to speak. "Now, shall we give your father the dignity he deserves?" Maria snapped.

Eva tried to be careful with the now stiffening body of her father but the weight of the body laid so much pressure on her already heavy body. Eventually she dragged her father into his freshly dug grave, with the help of her mother and grandmother. Leaving a trail behind him from where his body had lain. She felt sick as she touched his body, as it was cold and clammy. The smell of death penetrated her nose so deeply, she could taste it. This was not her father; she didn't recognize the person she was lifting. He was grey and gaunt, his fingernails black, cold and rigid. The earth clung to the clothes. He reminded her of a plastic doll that had not yet been painted. Slowly they lowered his body down into the earth, Eva shut down the emotions enveloping her, flooding through her veins. Her brain's defence mechanism switched to a more logical approach, it was easier to cope with. "He should have been burnt – no evidence." Eva whispered into the moist air to no one in particular, neither her grandmother nor her mother answered her – the statement was left unanswered.

Mechanically, the soil was returned to its original home, each taking their turn, no one spoke, each were bereft of emotion. The leaves were carefully laid out by hand, masking the mound of soil, carefully placed in an irregular pattern to disguise the grave.

Once complete, Maria, Faith and Eva nodded an unspoken agreement and silently began to walk back to the nearest thing Eva had thought of as a family home. The three women were so different in temperament, yet they were held together by a secret that had affected each of their lives so differently.

"Well madam, I think the time had come to relieve you of all those questions." Maria pointedly spoke to Eva.

2

Forty Years Earlier...

Maria sat with her head bent, leaning on her workstation. She gently massaged her eyes, with the back of her hands. They left the residue of salt tears as they glistened in the artificial light. Maria turned to her sink feeling the water run over her fingers washing away the tears, she was never sure what she had on them and safety always came first even subconsciously. She smiled to herself how everyone would laugh at her it they were here. She steadily stared down at her work goodness knows what she looked like. Her colleagues laughed not knowing what drove her to work so long hours especially with Jarvis always giving her a hard time. She didn't mind at least she felt like she was doing something that was useful – she had wanted to be on this project since she was a little girl.

A warm glow spread through Maria's body. She smiled as she looked at the view through the window – the sun was as red as ever, light danced over the inland sea, the shadow of the nearby mountain range gently marched its shadow over the low-lying land. That compared with her lab; metallic, sterile cupboards everywhere, nothing natural here. Then again, what was natural anymore? Those old photographs that her mother had shown her – her family, which was what exactly? They had smiled back at her, something that had now changed forever and it was something she would never have. Occasionally she dreamed of the old tales her mother had taught her: of Mother's, Father's, Grandparent's, sister's and brothers. A different time and place – another world.

With her still red smarting eyes, she turned from the

beautiful view that captivated her thoughts, glancing about her environment in which every item was so familiar to her.

The electronic posters caught her eye, more new policies from the Praeposters. A wry smile etched on her face, they reminded her of the paper documentation kept safe in the room opposite to where she worked daily. On her first day, Jarvis took her into that room, the hairs prickled all over her body, the dry paper crackled under her touch, slipped through her cotton clad fingers, everything was so precious, she was so lucky to have a brief glimpse of that unknown but oddly familiar world.

Old paper posters coiled tightly to protect them lay on shelves almost resembling a honeycomb. Stacked high in the corner plastic cartons containing silver disks and video tapes all the information just lying there made by what were they called – journalists. This alien concept now long since made redundant, fascinated by those long lost images of odd contraptions, tanks, helicopters, and there seemed to be a lot of sand on those silver disks. Jarvis was amazed she had showed interest in all that history – no one normally cared. Maria remembered sitting, looking through the posters calling for help, no one had expected the wars to change humanity, no one had expected the climate change so suddenly; lack of oil, humidity, terrorism, they found a way to change the civilized world.

Maria remembered reading, what had happened fully (for the first time). Her old history lessons had never focused on the reasons why but what came after. Using genetic modification of all the food sources were clever, disastrous, but clever. No one saw it coming. They just fought each other; they expected bombs, more destruction - not the ability to wipe out the males of the species. Genetics were hailed as the new cure for mankind, eradicating diseases. It eradicated men instead.

Maria had cried when she realized; watching the reports and reading the news stories – women all over the world disappearing as their sons were still born. It had not been long before the realization had struck those in power, that most men were sterile by their thirties. Of course they were the lucky ones they had a life, the world population had quartered, been decimated only one third had survived the last war. In her naivety, she couldn't believe all this information was hidden in a room at Genetics Control.

Tears rolled down her face as the full realization of the horror she was trying to rectify sank in. Posters were different now than the advertisements of the past. Of course, they were not allowed now. She knew the rest: children taken from their mothers to be protected, the floods, the world lay desolate, all this added to the despondent peoples around the world. Protecting the human race had become all important. It was this that had captivated her imagination as a child, that was why she needed to do something of use. It spurred her on in an endless tedium of statistics. She had told no one of that room – an unusual occurrence, as her bubbly nature hid nothing from her friends, regaling them of tales from work, so in depth they soon protested their boredom, not so the day she went into the dark recesses of history in 'the room' she didn't that day, nor since. They would not understand.

The poster flickered beaming a blue light deep into her lab bouncing off the white walls changing the image with what seemed to her more pointless information. She took no notice of its content but it brought her thoughts back to the test tubes before her. It had to change – it just had to.

Maria turned back to her work, ignoring the signs of

her tired body. The lights in front of the wall flickered indigo with numbers, different genes, and different specimens.

"New page - show me the chromosomes" Maria's voice had a monotone quality to it, as she directed the computer. Another page appeared on the wall – this time the figures were collated. Maria glanced at the flickering screen. How many specimens had they taken now? Each was now within the relays and circuits of the Mainframe computer.

"Computer report," Maria ordered the electronic brain; a third set of digits were projected in front of the wall. The chromosomes on each line showed the usual patterns, none carrying the Y gene. The flickering of ever changing digits abruptly stopped, one of the lines of figures were highlighted in yellow. Maria turned staring at the information highlighted, bile rose in her mouth, adrenalin raced through her body, excitement tingled in her fingers and toes. With shaking hands, she rubbed her eyes not quite believing what she saw. She couldn't help herself dancing like a child around the sharp objects of her lab. Loose strands of hair escaping from the tightly wound style she had so carefully pinned that morning.

"Calm Maria, Calm" she uttered aloud to herself.

"Wipe screening – leave analysis" Maria instructed the computer, "Enlarge defect." This couldn't be true it just couldn't. Sixty million specimens had gone into the data bank; she had been working on this for weeks, since leaving college, after her PhD. What would Jarvis say, quickly Maria examined the results there was definitely a naturally occurring Y, no manipulation, no splitting, not already badly formed. The life span of this would be normal. Not falsified and not genetically modified. Maria didn't know what to do first, did she contact Jarvis, head of the health department or even the head of the pyramid.

She didn't do any of the above, as her mind raced. She didn't wish to be made a fool of with Jarvis again – it would be a definite nightmare if she were wrong, that she could guarantee. It would be the end of her career as a biologist.

"Calm, think!" she muttered.

"Computer transfer data," breathing deeply Maria, made her decision "to my home." Maria needed to study this carefully and not with her superior questioning her every move. She had a feeling Jarvis would take the credit – this was not going to happen. Maria rushed around her lab tidying up all the information, quietly she wished private computers were allowed in here, but the contamination was such a risk with such an important research.

Wind swept her off her feet as she left the lab and its secrets, stepping onto the marble steps she inhaled the humid air. The lab was always set to an ambient temperature, she hated it. The warm air encompassed her reviving her body a few pink and purple streaks still lingered staining the dark blue sky. Steadily she walked to the hover depot. She really should have invested in her own but all the years at college had relieved her of any credits her mother had left her. She enjoyed the walk along the gently lapping sea. The cooler air whisping around her face.

The depot was quiet, she sat on the bench looking at the pristine white docking station; not a sole to disturb her thoughts, the masses left hours ago. She couldn't concentrate on the immense discovery she had made instead her friends would wonder where she had got to her normal routine of visiting them at the spring water café would have to wait. Her eyes involuntary closed she was still fighting her own exhaustion.

A low purr disturbed her sudden need of sleep, it became louder, interrupting the peace that surrounded her, the purple craft glided into the dock with the usual gust of wind blowing the last vestiges of Maria's now non-existent hairstyle out of place. Aching as she rose to her feet nudging the edges of her shoes shot pains up her young legs. Wincing she made her way to the open orange door of the hover, knowing within minutes she would be in the comfort of her home away from the sterile environment of her work and the pristine whiteness of the public streets.

She took her seat awaiting the familiar purr to start up again. Her stomach gave a jump it was a stupid idea sending her work home, she needed to verify this and fast. The consequences were dyer. It was too late now, her decision was made it would not take long to confirm the anomaly. While the mind flitted from excitement to fear, the hover gently took her home. Stopping outside her door, the chip in her wrist personal computer communicating silently with the hover. Maria walked onto the cracked pavement outside her vine covered apartment building. Each door opened to the footstep the tense feeling in her shoulders relaxed with each step taken.

Maria sat studying the information at her home; her personal computer chip for her house was out dated but it was friendly and she had had it since starting college – it was one of the few things she had kept from her mother. It had struggled with all the information she had transferred to it but even the computer knew the significance.

"Bring up sample – 4527985."

"It will be longer than expected would you like to shut down the kitchen to compensate?"

"Yes that will be fine – Oscar." Ceres always laughed at her – naming her computer. "It's inanimate" she would say on that regular basis but it was sometimes her only company and they fit.

"Complete" the wall flashed the name Vanessa Gresval. Maria thought they would need more tests just to prove this was not a fluke. The polynucleotide chains must have separated, why the hydrogen bonds must have been weaker in her deoxyribonucleic acid. Maria was lost in her own thoughts; what had happened? What had caused this? She had heard that the reproduction would rectify itself over time, but this quickly? It had only been a hundred years – this mutation must have happened for a reason.

The light started to creep along the skyline gently replacing the black blanket. Maria was running on adrenaline, she knew she would pay for being awake through the night, she could sleep later.

"Oscar communicate to my friend Ceres."

"Contacting her now," the metallic voice replied. Ceres appeared as a holographic image in front of her. Maria smiled to herself. Ceres looked as unkempt as usual, she was lucky no one at work ever commented about her appearance. Her mousey hair hung in rats tails down her back. Her redeeming feature was her eyes, they sparkled when she smiled, the hazel glint shone with the odd green flash as she got excited about her new crusade.

"Hi, Maria what's up?" She paused "Do you know how early it is?" Ceres moaned.

"Can you do me a favour?" Maria replied, "I would like you to check out a person, for me. Her name's Vanessa Gresval."

"Who's she?" Ceres inquired.

"Not sure – it's just something that's come up at work." Maria evaded Ceres' query – hoping she would not be too curious.

"Ok – I'll check the database. I might have to speak

to Erin and get her password." Ceres responded she knew Maria well it was probably another one of her schemes.

"Why? Do you not work in the programming department?" Maria sighed, "I'm not sure about Erin, as she's joined the pyramid; don't ask me why – I think she's too ambitious."

"This is from the woman who wishes to be the first, to find the missing gene!" Ceres laughed.

"Ok – just do what you have too, I need the information." The holographic image disappeared. Maria now totally exhausted, stiff in every muscle from sitting in the same position for hours now succumbed to the total exhaustion now controlling her body. Gingerly she pushed herself up and walked as if she were a zombie to her bed although her sofa was comfortable she seriously needed sleep. As an afterthought her words barely audible,

"Oscar, send word that I will be late in at the lab please."

"Consider it done" the mechanical voice responded to her request.

"Erin?" Ceres now stood as a holographic image on Erin's immaculate glass desk, everything had a place. It reflected Erin perfectly groomed her black hair pinned up, it would not dare to come out of place.

"Hi, what's the problem?" Erin answered her friend, her dark brown eyes sparked interest, she had been at work a while.

"Look I need a favour, can you get me – well Maria asked." Ceres paused; she knew she should be honest, Erin had not changed that much. Maria was always been suspicious of authority.

"Why did she not call me?" Erin interrupted.

"I don't think she thought it was your department" Ceres dismissed her friend's question as it was of no consequence. "Anyway what are you doing working on your own this early?" Ceres couldn't believe her friend's enthusiasm for her new position.

"I have to if I'm ever going to get promoted" Erin wrinkled her nose with distaste, "I'm fed up of doing all the boring jobs." Erin smiled "Anyway what do you and Maria want?"

"Oh, just can you get me an address of someone? Her name is Vanessa Gresval," Ceres answered.

"OK, I'll do it now, not to worry I'll let Maria know." Ceres turned to face the division screen, next to her she had better get on with some actual work. "I'll speak to you later, I'll meet you at Maria's after work." The image disappeared from Erin's desk.

"Computer, personnel database, home of Vanessa Gresval" a flat appeared on the division screen and an address appeared underneath it.

"Nice place" Erin recovered herself. "Occupation" Erin questioned the computer.

Engineer – Not bad, Erin thought, *I wonder what Maria wanted this for* – the communicator was not secure, Erin knew that much.

Erin downloaded the information into her personal handset. She then promptly deleted any record of the interference. In addition, Erin also deleted, where she had been in the network. A client was waiting for her in the interview room she didn't like to keep them waiting. She shrugged to herself it could wait until later although her interest had been piqued.

It had been a long day and feeling like a common criminal, which was stupidity as everyone at work used the information for their own devices, it was just the first time she had, it didn't sit right with her morals; she slowly headed towards Maria's home.

Maria had not moved since the death of the mother, it was not a great distance away, so after a short time of walking and being carried on the conveyor, Erin reached Maria's. Erin spoke into the intercom.

"Hi, it's Erin."

"Voice recognition activated" the metal disc on the wall answered. "Permission to enter." Erin hated where Maria lived, to call it lived in was an understatement. The cleaner was dysfunctional and the ancient intercom that she was so proud of, never was activated.

"Hi" Erin called to no one in particular, entering the space it had a look of a once glamorous flat now long gone but the feeling of the place was a magnet to most people. It didn't suit with Erin's taste. It was too prehistoric. In retrospect, the flat had the same dishevelled feel as its owner. It suited her totally; it was what she loved about her.

"We're in here" Ceres answered from the far corner, Maria and Ceres were in deep discussion; Maria's personal computer was off line. Erin followed their advice without anyone mentioning it and shut down her communicator; her position had made her suspicious by nature. Erin noticed their intimacy and felt jealous.

"So what's the matter of urgency?"

Ceres laughed "Maria's only gone and found the missing link."

"What! Why doesn't everyone know? God, you will be famous!" Erin was pleased for her friend; she knew this was what Maria had wanted all her life.

"I don't think so, I need to make sure of what I have found before I go public" Maria replied, self depreciatingly.

"Are you mad? You will be honoured, hailed as a hero - imagine, no more lotteries, god I am dreading that." Erin twittered and was amazed at the news.

"What are you talking about Praeposter's never get picked – or had you not worked that out?" Ceres said, "You amaze me, you join the very people that rule with no democracy and you have no clue how they work."

"Oh for my sake shut up, no politics" Maria interrupted. She had been there many times before.

"But democracy doesn't work – look at the last Great War. Useless and you have been reading all those banned notes, of the centuries ago again – I could get into serious trouble for being friends with you – anyway who wants to be poor an idealist." Erin fingered the large diamond on her finger.

"Just shut up Erin and don't you butt in either," Ceres and Erin both rolled their eyes conspiratorially. Maria had that affect on them but they both were quiet – she mothered both of them.

"Did you get the information I asked for?" Maria steering the conversation back to its original subject.

"Yes, so you want me to download it?" Erin replied slightly chastised.

"No I want to meet her – I need some answers - mainly why her?" Maria fell back into her reverie excluding the others in the room, she returned to her work in her mind. "She needs to have a full examination and hopefully her genes will get rid of those awful enclosures."

"Do you really believe that?" Erin asked perplexed "I'm not so sure"

"She has got to go public, imagine the credit we would get, this woman will have to be inseminated she will have to," Ceres stated.

Maria quietly said "to have it taken away – we do that to murderers, thieves and assassins. I don't think she'll agree to this, so I've got to be careful."

"You are just over reacting and listening to Ceres too much, it will be fine." Erin was convinced that the people she worked for were worth more than her friends gave them credit for.

"This is the lady who spies for a living – a good incentive!" Ceres said with sarcasm.

"Look, are we going to go or talk about it? I need this information and I don't want to explore it at work." Maria got up to leave, Ceres and Erin followed sulking, as chastised schoolchildren.

3

Maria, Ceres and Erin caught a hover to the other side of the city. Erin was impressed. It was where she had always wanted to live. The streets were tree-lined and they overlooked the sea – many of the higher-ranking officials in the pyramid lived in this area.

"I'm going to live here – one day," Erin mused to herself.

"It will be probably out of fashion by the time you can afford one of these – do you only think of money?" Ceres accused her.

"No, but it helps" she paused "we all can be idealistic and poor, I chose to be idealistic on some things but I am afraid where my comfort is concerned I am extremely realistic." Maria was ignoring their friendly banter, as she studied where they were.

"I think we are nearly there." She looked up at the large block of concrete in front of her – glass everywhere with sections on the building looking as if it belonged to another age. Erin walked up to the door.

"Vanessa Gresval – please."

"Voice recognition denied – confirm name"

"Erin Holt" the voice that replied was not the computer.

"Hello – can I help?"

"Is that Vanessa?" Erin replied

"Yes – who are you?"

"As I said Erin Holt, I've also got my colleagues here, Maria Stevenson and Ceres Zanuti," Erin stated. Feeling as though she should explain further she continued. "We are from the preposter department at the central pyramid."

"I'm sorry to be rude but what do you want?" Maria

carefully ushered Erin aside.

"Do you remember taking a specimen, around four years ago?" Maria asked tentatively, she knew everyone became suspicious when dealing with preposters.

"Yes" Vanessa answered apprehensively.

"Well, I've found an anomaly with yours – I've come here to discuss it with you – I'd prefer not to discuss it on your doorstep."

"Why have you not gone through official channels?" Vanessa was not convinced.

"I wanted to do this quickly, although my friend Erin is a monitor. You can check our credentials." Maria held her breath; they waited in silence as each second ticked by.

"Come in." Obviously, Vanessa had checked out their identities via the communicator, as the door opened automatically. Relieved and apprehensive they stepped into the lift, immediately they were taken to Vanessa's floor. All three women were nervous. Erin didn't like this, she couldn't understand why they were here, and surely, this was for the authorities, not for them to interfere in policies, however Maria was insistent.

The lift eventually stopped, A small dark haired women with piercing blue eyes obviously Vanessa, opened the inner door to her apartment; revealing a spacious apartment, Erin glanced around the room this must be beautiful in daylight. The floor-length glass windows ran along one wall cream sofas were placed in the centre nothing was out of place except for the toy strewn corner, just as Erin had seen via her computer. Vanessa was not alone an exceptionally pretty little girl with black hair and bright green eyes was playing in the corner.

"I am sorry about the mess – Natasha is causing

havoc – she's at that age' Vanessa turned to her daughter with a look of pride and love – "Excuse my manners you must understand we need to be careful."

Erin and Ceres didn't say anything to Maria but both looked sceptical.

"Hi, my name is Maria Stevenson," Maria held out her hand, "and this is Erin and Ceres" both women added their greeting, without giving away too many misgivings.

"Nice to meet you" replied Vanessa. "Please take a seat." They all sat down each feeling uncomfortable. Vanessa apprehensively watched her daughter play with her toys.

"Well" Maria started; she had, had this conversation rehearsed in her head and as usual, she had gone blank. "I'm from the research of biotechnology – Genetics control," she introduced her subject officially "As you may have seen on the news comm. – we have been researching the possibility of having genes tested for what we would call abnormal, but in fact would be normal in our evolution, obviously this would be before the war." Maria paused hoping Vanessa would guess why she was here – she was wrong.

"So - what's all this got to do with me?" Vanessa asked 'let us be honest I have been through the lottery and look what I've got - a perfectly healthy little girl."

"Yes, I can see that – but I would like to double check my findings" Maria replied.

"OK, I'll come to the lab for the tests next week, before then I'm unable to get someone to look after my daughter." Vanessa was not bothered by the idea – but Maria was horrified.

"That would be great but I need to analyse this soon - as we may have a bit of a discovery" she looked quite pleased for herself, in a innocent sort of way this grabbed Vanessa's normally hard faced feelings, toward her. "I'm sorry to be a bit premature but I have brought with me a specimen tube I was hoping you would be able to give me something today, so I would be able to continue my research tomorrow."

"What would I have to do?" Vanessa never trusted doctors at any time, but an academic was worse.

"Oh not to worry, I just need a hair from your head, it has the entire DNA I need." Maria replied seeing Vanessa's resistance.

"Oh if that's all," Vanessa seemed relieved, Maria put on the gloves that were in her pocket as gently as possible, she tugged the hair from Vanessa's head.

"Ow!" Vanessa exclaimed, her hand automatically went to her head, where Maria had removed the hair. Maria had not noticed, she was too busy examining the hair to see if the follicle was attached. She placed them carefully inside the tube and placed it carefully back in her pocket. Natasha started to cry and Erin thought it was time they left. You didn't get apartments in this side of town for nothing, her mind raced with how many favours Vanessa had granted to achieved such a prestigious address, her instincts were telling her there was more to this than it first seemed, she had worked for the pyramid long enough to know that.

They were ushered out, with a plethora of thank yous from Maria and relief from Erin and Ceres – none of them said anything as they headed home each to their own apartments. Maria knew that both Ceres and Erin, although supportive of her, thought she was wrong in her findings. The news comm. constantly informed everyone of the slow struggle of the development. No one really cared and continued with their own lives, what difference would it make to the masses – but her results were telling her different. She nearly skipped home and couldn't wait to tell Polly in the morning of the exciting news.

4

The laboratory was unusually busy, as it was normal for her to work late in the evening no one questioned her, as the others got ready to leave. Maria sat at her bench secretly watching her colleagues; as she pretended to look through the specimens, checking for any discrepancies, feeling a fraud, as she knew of at least one. She had volunteered for this job that morning hoping no one would query her motives. It was always the last job to be taken, as it was tedious. There could have been many discrepancies, but Maria would not have noticed today; normally very precise in everything she did, she could neither concentrate on what she was doing nor could she think of what she needed to do this evening.

"Bye... Lock up before you leave." Polly said with a glint in her eye.

"Don't worry; I'll shut down the lab system before I leave tonight." Maria replied trying to make light as the joke was intended.

"It was a good job I needed to be here early, or you could have been in some serious trouble," Polly said concerned for her colleague's welfare.

"I'll be fine – you get yourself off home or your mother will have your dinner waiting." Maria laughed hoping it sounded genuine – it was their favourite joke. Her mother was constantly contacting her via the communicator. It sometimes made her feel pleased she was an orphan but as always, the guilt enveloped her.

"Yes I'd better had." With that, Polly gave Maria an affectionate hug and went out of the lab door.

Maria shut her eyes she was no good at this – her friends always accused her of being transparent. The sun shone brightly through the window she just stared out over the sea. With a jolt, she realized she had been staring into space for an hour. Maria walked over to the sink splashing water over her face. She needed to be alert when she ran these tests. Gently she took out a small tube out of her pocket putting it on the bench. Carefully removing the strand of hair, she put it in the sampler.

"Computer run program 397" a low hum emitted from the cylindrical case. Slowly time ebbed away, although Maria checked the time so regularly she could have sworn it was going backwards.

"Program complete" Maria startled, jumped up from her seat.

"Show results" she commanded; the light played on the wall slowly forming the figures and digits to confirm the results Maria saw previously. Almost falling into her seat exhausted and relieved. Maria let herself have one small smile as flickering, on the wall before her, were the same results. It was not her mind playing tricks with her. The results didn't change. Her mind silently exulted with her find. Slowly the feeling of silent euphoria died down.

If this was the correct results, as it seemed to be. Why? If Vanessa had been through the program, why had she conceived a girl? Maria's mind raced.

She felt sick at what she thought; she hoped so much it was not. *Could it be a simple fifty, fifty chance that her work was not for nothing?* She hoped not, doubt seeped through the electrodes in her brain, she needed proof.

"Computer – have all the samples been checked?" She knew they should not have been not according to her senior, that was why she was here.

"Yes" Maria felt there was an explosion in her head, she became hot and clammy, and her breathing was

32

getting faster. *Think, Maria think,* she thought to herself.

"Computer – please check for other specimens with the same discrepancies as this specimen, then please list." She stated trying to keep her voice level and calm.

She sat starring at the blank wall in front of her what seemed to be hours – she waited and waited.

"New program complete" Maria watched in horror as the different specimens lit up the lab scrolling one page after the other. A quick mental calculation of the page numbers over half of the women tested could have children naturally and most likely capable of having an Y embryo.

"Computer state how many specimens in the data base in total." She didn't want the answer.

"Ten million" she was horrified at the implications, she needed proof and fast. *Why and who?*

"Transfer the new program, including the accompanying results - to my home." She said "then delete the new program," her gut instinct yesterday had been proved right but what was she going to do now. Slowing and with random thoughts she slowly and methodically tided up – there would be no mistakes this evening. She was pleased it was a rest day tomorrow – she couldn't face anyone.

"Lights off" she paused wondering if what happened in this small room would change her life forever. Maria wondered if it was best not to say a word, shrugging that idea as quickly as it had come, her own morality would not let her. Who was she kidding of course it would.

"Shut down connection" The door shut behind her.

The three of them sat – all their beliefs had been ripped from them – none doubted Maria now, but only after, they had been shown the results. No one spoke Erin sat quietly she had taken this the hardest of all. Looking over to her friend, she always had Ceres and her conspiracy theories; Erin was secretly horrified what Ceres had been preaching to anyone who would listen had been proven correct. It meant she had been leading a life that was a lie.

Maria was worried about Erin she had always defended her belief in the system it had come as a complete shock.

"What's the proof you need it could be in front of you - it could be that woman you work for, she might not have told anyone" Erin, said not believing herself. Just trying to find reasons, any except the obvious.

"Don't be absurd" Ceres butted in Do you honestly believe that. Look who works there – Maria newly out of college, no family. Polly lovely but a bit dim, Dina couldn't care less and is obsessed with her appearance, do I need to go on?" Ceres paused "these are people who are handpicked by the pyramid. No offence Maria but didn't you say that woman who left, has changed her career – Why?"

"Apparently – she was good at her job." Maria replied, "She wanted to work outside the constraints of the lab environment; I think she's in construction now."

"Maybe too good." Ceres said, "what are you going to do?"

"I don't know" Maria said, "think I need to get into the institute, there's a genetic department attached to obstetrics"

"What are you talking about? You will end up in front of the pyramid" Erin was horrified she had heard the horror stories at work. She couldn't believe that her most law abiding friend, was seriously considering breaking the guidelines. If it had been Ceres, she could have understood.

34

"I need my name in the lottery I've got to get in there" Maria mused over her ideas, not really talking to anyone.

"You can't, you're too young," Erin answered automatically. Ceres said agreeing with Erin.

"I could transfer, like my predecessors and not say anything." Maria said.

"Too obvious," Ceres said, "someone might get suspicious"

"You will probably find your actions are being monitored anyway – that make's Ceres and me suspects too."

"Look, I don't want to get you in trouble, you're just visiting a friend," Maria replied diverting Erin's fears "I mean you've been friends with Ceres for years and that's not hindered you getting in the pyramid." Maria broadly grinned at her friend, she felt like she had not smiled for weeks not days.

"Ok – what do you actually want to do with this information?" Erin asked ever practical.

"I was thinking of putting it on the net." Maria said.

"But it's archaic – it would never get passed by the Praeposter's." Erin stated.

"And no one uses it anymore" Ceres said agreeing with Erin.

"Precisely – or so the Praeposter's think they are really lapse with it and yes there are people out there who use it . I've been on it" Maria stated "look you know what those enclosures are like if the information I've got is correct they are taking the chromosome from the sperm. That also means the men don't die naturally– they must be killing them off." Maria finished airing her view. "Besides it would soon spread through the population, we all love a good gossip".

"Have you been on an overdose of imagination?" Ceres said.

"No but sperm deteriorates severely overtime it's always been harder for women to get pregnant later – that's why the lottery only takes women from twenty to twenty five – it should be earlier but most think college is important so the polices changed to incorporate that," Maria nodded.

"We know this – but murdering the males – Why?" Erin didn't like this; her gut feeling was indicating Maria could be on to something terrifying.

"The Praeposter's – you see that on the News Comms – it's about Power" Maria was frustrated "Don't you two ever read history books – after the war we had biological weapons, what happened to the men's genetics was temporary, it has already corrected itself – we've had no wars since the men were in the institutions – will you two think!"

"You are making the case for the pyramid" Erin said, "Will you back me up Ceres – she's been listening to you too long"

"It does seem far-fetched, I've been ranting about democracy for years – don't say it, I know you don't think it works" Ceres got up off the sofa looking out over the city. "You know I join these groups – well one of the women was a guard. She mentioned that the males think they are to retire in a separate part of the complex – they don't – they're incinerated" Ceres paused, neither Maria nor Erin spoke. "See it is to keep the number down – apparently it started about forty years ago I was sworn to secrecy but it was a joke she kept telling anyone who would listen – we all thought she was slightly mad – hey maybe not!" Ceres pulled out of her pocket a packet of cigarettes and lit one. She inhaled deeply.

"For god sake – come away from the window you will have me arrested" Maria said disapprovingly.

"Anyway" Ceres said, as she did what Maria asked

blowing out blue smoke around the room. They are injected with insulin, an overdose, some are kept alive but not long. They have shocks but it is done with their own DNA so it matches perfectly, so she said. It keeps the theory that the genetic modification for the Y chromosome is defective." Silence filled the room Erin and Maria were both horrified. It was ok to have a suspicion but to have it confirmed. "So much for her being in a mental institution, I cannot believe she actually might be telling us the truth all that time."

"This needs to be broadcast across the network." Maria was incensed.

"So you think old system at the net will achieve this, we need to publish it on the news comms." Erin said, "these males are dying for no reason" Erin looked at her friends "what was her name?"

"I don't know" – she disappeared after two weeks we thought she had been institutionalised." Ceres answered, "I'm sorry Maria I don't think we dare get the extra information you need – it's too dangerous. I think what you have, will have to do. They will blame us for keeping the information from the pyramid it's too risky I need the proof" Maria didn't know if she was up to this - neither did Ceres or Erin, it was so much bigger than any one of the three young women had thought all straight from college and their naivety shattered forever.

5

"Natasha, come here – darling" Vanessa called to her daughter. A small child of six came towards her; her nearly black hair glinted in the sunlight – that streamed through the window.

"What's the matter Mummy?"

"Nothing darling I just wanted a cuddle" Vanessa stroked her daughter's hair amazed how quickly it grew.

"Have I done something to upset you?" Natasha's lower lip trembled. "I don't want to upset you" She threw her arms around her mother's neck.

"Oh, sweet heart – I was only joking" Vanessa pulled her daughter in a tight embrace. She had not been happy since those women had paid her a visit – Maria yes that was her name but she couldn't remember the names of the women who came with her. She realized that she had wanted her DNA but why? What was this anomaly? Something was warning her - this was not right, her gut instinct was playing a concerto in her stomach. The more she thought about it the more frightened she got – Vanessa knew what the Praeposter's could be like. If it was just herself she would not have cared but since the lottery (she felt it was a disaster at the time) she was not going to risk her life or her daughters. The pyramid would think she had helped them.

"In what?" She muttered.

"What Mummy?" her sleepy daughter asked.

"Nothing darling – I just spoke aloud my thoughts nothing to worry about Natasha." The apartment felt claustrophobic she needed to get out.

"Natasha go and get your coat – I think it's too early for you to have a nap" Vanessa needed out and now she needed to make a decision and she definitely needed a clear head.

"Aww, Mummy do I have to?" Natasha was moaning, she snuggled into her mother, she liked sitting on her mother's knee since she had gone back to work, she was always tired. Vanessa put her down disgruntled, Natasha's shoulders slumped, feeling petulant she kicked out at the chair.

"Come on let us go to the beach." Vanessa stated seeing her daughter's unhappiness. Natasha smiled it sounded like a good deal; she scampered off to get her coat.

Vanessa walked through the dappled shade of the trees – she walked listening to the waves lapping against the pebbled beach.

"Mummy I'm hot"

"It's alright darling the rainy season will be here soon." Vanessa replied trying to comfort her.

"At school last week we were learning about the Earth's gravitational pull." Natasha wanted to impress her mother – she wanted her mother to think she was clever; she liked being the best at school.

"Yes? And did you learn anything about Europe's weather?" Vanessa asked.

"I didn't know the climate wasn't always like this. It was different when there were men." Natasha said, impressed her mother asked her a question, she always seemed so clever. It was lucky she had specialised in this subject last week.

"There still are men, darling" Vanessa interrupted.

"I know but we don't see them anymore, do we? Anyway from what we have learnt in history they seem very frightening" Natasha paused unsure what to say next "they caused all sorts of trouble – didn't they Mummy?"

"Not necessarily – we have learnt a lot since the war, anyway you were telling me about the climate" Vanessa laughed, indulging her daughter was her favourite pastime.

"Well the magnetic pull of the earth has changed – did you know that?" Natasha carried on not waiting for an answer, she felt it was very important that her Mummy had asked so many questions.

"This was called Britain and we used to get snow!" Natasha's eyes lit up "Can you imagine that Mummy – Snow!" Vanessa was secretly pleased, the school informed her that Natasha had a high IQ – she must have been lucky with the genes. Her thoughts wandered what if Maria was right. *What it she could carry this rare gene?*

"Mummy – why has our world changed so much?" Before Vanessa could answer her daughter rambled on "I know everything is blamed on the war – but can't we put it right again?" Vanessa couldn't believe it was if she was reading her thoughts.

"I don't know Natasha"

"From what Kate says at school – the men were horrible – sending missiles and things to us."

"Your teacher should give you an overall view of what happened not a biased one. There were males that helped and looked after women and children they were kind I wish they would not use this propaganda at schools." Vanessa replied.

"What's propaganda Mummy?" Natasha asked, having never heard the word before.

"Nothing darling I was just thinking aloud again please forget I ever said it." Vanessa said startled at herself for even saying that, never mind outside.

"But Mummy why are they in enclosures if they are like us – I thought they were scary?" Natasha asked not letting the subject drop.

"No darling, without those enclosures and the careful monitoring of the species we all would have been extinct years ago." Vanessa tried to answer her daughter – not knowing herself. She didn't like where her thoughts were taking her.

"Oh - Can we go and see them?" Natasha asked.

"No - Natasha not yet." Bored with the conversation and not interested in its implications, Natasha ran towards the edge of the waves with her black hair trailing behind her.

Vanessa couldn't help thinking if what she was about to do was right. The little girl dancing in the surf was the only important thing in her life and she must protect her at all costs it didn't make the decision any easier. The large pyramid loomed in the distance, shrugging her shoulders Vanessa walked towards it.

"Natasha come on," she shouted over to Natasha still playing in the waves.

Vanessa glanced up towards the large glass pyramid precariously built on a headland as if it rose out of the sea. The sun's rays reflected out towards her. She didn't notice its beauty just a chill ran through her.

"Natasha come close now." She called to her daughter her happy face betrayed what Vanessa felt inside. The fear was palpable as her daughter ran towards her. She grabbed hold of her hand as if she could lose her any second and started the climb up the marble steps toward the infernal building, in which most tried to avoid all their lives.

"Hello can I speak to a monitor please?" Vanessa was standing in the reception area of the Pyramid. The computer interface answered her with an enquiry.

"Any particular person or reason?"

"Yes, but I would prefer to speak to someone about this, I am not sure if it is anything at the moment." Vanessa had still not completely convinced herself it was the right thing to do.

"A monitor will be with you in a moment." Vanessa saw two seats appear out of the nearby wall, as there was no one else here she presumed it was for herself and Natasha.

"Come on darling we'll sit down here." Vanessa and Natasha made themselves as comfortable as possible while they waited.

"Intercom," flashed on Erin's computer, hardly anyone was in the office as most were working at home or out on surveillance.

"Yes?" Erin asked the computer

"We have a Vanessa Gresval in reception could you interview her as your diary is free." It just couldn't be, suddenly Erin's palms felt water logged in the cool atmosphere of the air conditioned building.

"I'm sorry but I need to finish my work." She replied.

"But your diary is free" the computer answered her "If you are working it should be logged." Terror pulsed through her veins.

"I will rectify it," she snapped.

"Could another monitor do it? I really need to finish this work" Erin was starting to panic now. What if she was recognized and what if Maria said was true? She could do with knowing what was said, in that meeting. "I'll watch you, as you always need a watcher anyway and I can get my work completed as well."

"This is not conformance but it will do" Erin sighed with relief. "Please transfer report to watcher room 3." Erin left her desk and walked along the corridor to her hidden chamber.

The door into the empty room was open through the glass she could see the other chamber – her's was sparse and uncomfortable unlike the one she was looking at. Softly furnished and painted a soft green overlooking the gardens outside. It could be anyone's living space she thought to herself, as she watched three people enter the room. Vanessa and her daughter followed by a colleague Georgina. Erin sat hoping it was about something different to what she thought.

"Please take a seat" Georgina asked them both "would your daughter like to play on the computer?" Erin smiled word perfect as they were taught in college. Natasha's eyes lit up and she was bored anyway, she had thought they would be at the beach all day but as usual, her mother had something else to do. She felt life was not fair. On the small table in front of her appeared a small holographic chess set Natasha's attention was diverted from her mother as she tried to battle with the mainframe. "Now how can I help you?" Georgina asked thinking it was another waste of her time.

"Well I think this is going to sound silly" Vanessa paused now thinking she was over reacting and not at all comfortable in here shifting in her seat. I had a visit from three people they said they were lab technicians – I think or they could have been something else they had all the relevant identification and stuff" Vanessa thought she sounded like a moron now and from the look on Georgina's face she did too. Erin unseen from Vanessa felt sick she hoped Georgina would think it was a crank caller. "Well these women said they'd found an anomaly with my DNA and I was unsure whether to believe them or not and then they said I could help the human race as they think I carry the Y gene. I know they kept them frozen at the enclosures but I didn't believe her when she first said this, but the more she went on about it the more plausible it sounded." Vanessa paused for breath. "Well I was never much good at biology, I am an engineer you see." She could see she was not making much sense.

"Do you feel these people (you never gave me the

names?) Have invaded your privacy?" Georgina asked hoping what this woman was saying would become clearer, as she had no idea what she was talking about. Erin held her breath they all could be ruined.

"Yes I think they did, I don't believe that this anomaly exists, or it would have been transmitted." Vanessa started feeling stronger, but still covering her back. "However, not thinking I let her take a piece of my hair and a swab from my mouth. At first, I thought it was a good idea but then once I had time to think about it I am unsure. I was worried that it was a gang using my DNA for unauthorised reasons. Which is why I came to you, I don't want my daughter at risk."

"Yes we have heard of unscrupulous gangs trying to use these deceptive measures for unauthorised use." Georgina answered her hoping she might be a bit more forthcoming with the information. "You said that there was a leader; do remember her name or any of the other's. Erin paused from trying to finish her report and watched as she tried to remember the name of the woman behind the mirror.

"Oh yes the name of the leader was Maria Stevenson" Erin felt as if she were going to faint.

"And the others?" Georgina asked. Erin waited with baited breath.

"I'm sorry; the only thing I remember is that the first names both had very short names." Vanessa sighed, it was a huge relief – she had done it.

"Is there anything else you can remember it may help?"

"I'm sorry no – I think I need to get my daughter home now."

"Yes of course" Georgina answered "we will keep you informed of the investigation, if anyone comes again please don't hesitate to contact me."

"Natasha" the chess set vanished and Natasha ran

over to her mother, "Come on let's go – I think we will do something special tonight." Vanessa left the room and made her way out of the building. Georgina watched her go out of earshot.

"Well, what did you think?" She turned asking the mirror "Mirror clear." Georgina asked. "Where has she got to?" She asked aloud, as the sparsely furnished room had no sign of habitation.

"Communicator" Erin stated, "Get me Maria Jane Stevenson she works at the biotech lab." Erin sat at her desk sweat was pouring down the crease in her back.

"Hi, how are you? My projects nearly finished" there was no answer from Erin "What's wrong?" Maria felt a chill run down her spine.

"Get rid of it – get rid of it now..." grasping the chair beside her. Erin never brought her work home, what was she going to say how would she get out of work?

Erin slumped in her chair. "Erase message from mainframe."

"Erin Holt" the computer butted into her thoughts Maria had disappeared no long conversations today.

"Your vitals' are irregular is one having palpitations?"

"I am fine; I may need to leave soon."

"I can organise a consultation, it will only take a nano second."

"It is not necessary; I will rest at home I have been working too hard recently."

"Odd my database does not confirm your statement but if rest is what you need I will log your absence as unwell".

"Thank you" Erin relaxed only slightly, her door suddenly opened.

"Where did you get to interesting wasn't it? Should make a reasonable report let's hope we can follow this up" Georgina was standing in front of the vision wall not looking at the disconnection notice still visible behind her. *(Keep her talking)* Erin thought to herself. "Sorry I had work to finish, so I came up here once they had left" Disconnection to Maria Stevenson was flashing on the wall behind Georgina.

"You must be keen. Anyway come on, I need your help you have always been better at writing reports than I have." Georgina gushed; Erin was irritated she was always so lazy.

"What's your rush I didn't think anything was that unusual?" Erin answered.

"Well I've been digging and I found this Maria and she works at biotech." Georgina paused looking pleased with herself "I reckon she's found the anomaly, it looks like we will have to get rid of this one too."

"What anomaly?" Erin not being part of the Preposter's for long, she didn't have the background of her colleague, who had been with them five years who had not risen within the pyramid, as her laziness was common knowledge.

"'You know the deception; we had to get rid of one before you came – we thought she was going public." Georgina's face sneered "idiots if you ask me"

"Complete" the computer broke the tension Erin knew she was supposed to know what she was supposed to do, but this, she felt sick. What they had thought must be true and it was common knowledge within the pyramid if junior levels such as herself, were allowed to know.

"Come on let us get this done then." Erin told the woman who had just thrown her life in turmoil. She needed to get to Maria without making it obvious. *It will take a while but how?*

6

Maria was standing in the communal rest room, the garbled message from Erin had scared her into doing the one thing she should not do – nothing. Unsteady on her feet she sat down on the uncomfortable stools (they were to encourage productivity – not breaks). Having shocks had become quite the habit ironically, she thought she should be used to them by now. Maria knew Erin had warned her someone would find out, she knew if her suspicions were correct she would have, the Praeposter's following her. She couldn't contact any of her friends someone would know she would have told them *think Maria think* she whispered to herself she knew she relied on her friends too often; she was on her own now.

"I've told you before you are not allowed communication whilst at work Maria." Jarvis had walked in on her, whilst her thoughts were scattered. It took a second for her to register the situation.

"I'm sorry – a friend is in trouble I need to help her." Maria saw Jarvis was not going to be moved. "I'll make up the time this weekend." Maria crossed her fingers behind her back it could go either way.

"What's wrong with her?" Jarvis asked abruptly. Maria panicked – randomly she saw a broken file on the floor.

"She's broken her leg – fell over on the conveyor" Maria smiled benignly although it didn't quite reach her eyes. Erin had always called her for being a useless liar – she could always tell with her eyes. You would never make a good monitor she had said; Jarvis was silently appraising her employee.

"It's never happened before and I know you work over a lot – go on, get out of here before I change my mind."

"Thanks Jarvis – I won't forget this." Maria walked quickly she knew time was running out. She didn't dare to run, it would make it obvious, God *Erin give me more time.*

"I think we should go after the leak," Georgina stated as she leant on Erin's desk. This irritated Erin intensely, although it didn't show at all.

"Not yet it may be a hoax, I think this should be reported to someone higher in the pyramid." Erin replied.

"Oh come on I need that promotion and you are only starting out. It'll look really good on our reports" Georgina's eyes gleamed at the thought of having a big case, she was good at following the rules but didn't have the intelligence to make up her mind fully and always went running to superiors. She needed to prove she could control the situation and needed to prove it with this case.

"Look Georgina, I want to examine what this? What's her name?" Erin paused delaying for time.

"Vanessa Gresval"

"Anyway" Erin couldn't believe how immature Georgina was; it was no wonder her superiors had never promoted her. She hoped she could pull off the half-formed idea of a plan within her mind although with a distinct distaste at her colleague she may cause trouble through her lack of mental ability.

"I need to examine her past and also her colleagues at Biotech, surely you must agree?" Erin made it more of a statement than a question. Georgina had her usual look of being unsure. Erin half smiled maybe Georgina being a massive idiot could help the situation. Erin knew she could play for time; she didn't want to have to arrest her best friend.

"Ok you know she's at biotech but why would she go to Vanessa and who are the others?" Erin wiped her hands on her trousers; they always got sweaty when under pressure, she had to keep it as close to the truth as possible – it made a better lie.

"I tell you what, I will go and check out biotech and interview this Maria," Georgina said.

"That sounds like a good idea; while you are there I'll ask the mainframe to check the programs to see if they've been corrupted." Georgina jumped off the desk and turned abruptly.

"What about the report on the interview? Shouldn't we do that first" She asked.

"Of course, why don't you get on with that and be clear on your facts and I'll check the mainframe, as I said if you wait I'll be back in time for both of us to get to the lab." Erin hoped that this sounded like this was normal procedure; she knew they were supposed to have two people together, when there was an occurrence.

"That sounds great; it'll give me more time before we let the superiors know." Erin sighed; she had to get to Ceres quickly.

Erin walked outside the main headquarters of the pyramid. Everything Maria had said was true, what did it make her? She knew what was going on and this was disgusting. No matter how bad these creatures were, they couldn't be locked up like this then killed off one by one. She needed Ceres' help this was not going to happen and she knew Ceres well enough and her conspiracy theories, raising her wrist she spoke quietly into her personal communicator.

"Ceres Zanuti"

"Hi, Erin how are you?" Ceres said sounding

relieved, that someone had interrupted her at work.

"Fine, I can't talk over the communicator" Erin paused "meet me at mine in fifteen minutes."

"What's the matter?" Ceres asked.

"I said I couldn't talk, it's Maria" Erin sighed, "Communication complete."

Erin knew her living space was easier to get to for both of them and time was running out. She couldn't be too long Georgina would get suspicious. Ceres had the security code to her apartment, as they all did for each other. Erin waited for her to turn up. Pacing the main area of her space she formulated a plan there was no way she could help Maria and she wondered honestly how committed to her work she would be, there may be some good that had come from this it had to.

"Hi, I thought Maria would be here" Ceres said walking into the space. "Hey have you changed the colour of this?" It was painted in pale turquoise, as always although it was small it was always up to date.

"Yes, it is not important" Erin snapped, "Vanessa went to the Praeposter's there was only me and Georgina in the office, so I got to listen to the conversation"

"God did she see you?" Ceres looked horrified.

"No, I watched" Ceres looked at her quizzically "Don't ask my position is tentative as it is. Maria has been named, but we have not. I cannot be seen with her at all, so I need you to get a message to her somehow, one of your contacts or something." Ceres stood she didn't move at all. Erin just carried on she didn't have time to watch over any one. "Are you listening I need your full attention none of this will change anything and you going into shock will not help Maria." Ceres sat and nodded not saying a word. "Right Can you get a message to Maria that will be secure." Ceres nodded again. "Good, I'd prefer it if you didn't go yourself but it might be safer. I need all of Maria's project on paper"

"That is illegal, we could be caught and be in more trouble." Ceres interrupted her - the shock now wearing off.

"It has to be so we can keep it," Erin replied. "As there has been a security breach they will make it impossible for us to get it. We need that so Maria does not get such a high sentence. I cannot protect her. What we spoke about the other day well all the theories we got right. They've got rid of one of the biologists already and its common knowledge within the pyramid – it made me sick, Georgina who is as low as I am told me."

"Someone must have leaked it before" Ceres replied.

"I told you they tried, I know Maria was only doing her job but it will be misconstrued and she will come to the same fate as the other girl. Don't ask, I don't know." She saw that Ceres was about to ask what had happened. To her, they didn't have time.

"Anyway if we get this on paper and we can get one of your organisations behind it, it might work as blackmail, I don't know. I presume this goes all the way to the top." Erin was thinking aloud she worked far better like this having someone to bat her ideas off.

"I'll go with Maria she must be terrified have you spoken to her?" Ceres asked.

"Yes. Not sufficiently though I sent a garbled message as Georgina came into my office. I had to cut off the communication. I am hoping she is out of work, she needs to sort herself out. I am going to have to go and investigate this I will try to stall Georgina as long as possible but I am hoping you have enough time. Don't be seen with her and I will keep you informed.

I am sorry Ceres but you are going to have let Maria know that they will arrest her. Even though she has not managed to get anything done as yet, just her job." Erin hugged her friend they needed to be strong Erin felt sick that she was letting her friend take this responsibility; Maria would not harm anyone and she knew in her heart they would blame her she couldn't avoid it and if she could, she didn't know how.

"Take care of yourself." Erin gave a weak smile to her friend. "Don't blame yourself – we knew as soon as Maria brought that work home she was in trouble. You know how the Praeposter's work more than any of us." Ceres tried to reassure Erin. She could see it made her feel responsible.

"If I thought I knew how they worked I am mistaken. I don't know whom I am angrier at, me for being so assured and proven terribly wrong or Maria for being so naive. Any way get off – my cover is seeing you lot - to see if she breached any passwords – this we already know – she didn't." Ceres went leaving Erin to cover for her friend and hoping they succeeded, and she didn't.

What was going to happen to them all?

7

"Maria it's only me" Ceres called as she walked into Maria's apartment. "Maria!" Ceres shouted again.

"What are you doing here? Hasn't Erin spoken to you? I don't know what's going on but I've got a really nasty feeling about all this." Maria had obviously been crying her eyes were puffy and red. Ceres didn't know how she was going to do this.

"Do you want a drink?" She asked putting off the inevitable.

"Cut the crap, what's going on?" Maria snapped, totally out of character.

"Erin has given me instructions and I think it's the only way around this." She took a deep breath and hoped she would take this better than Ceres expected. "Vanessa has been to the Praeposter's and the only person's name she could remember was yours. They have traced you at biotech and Erin was saying they were saying it is a conspiracy, everyone knows at the pyramid." Ceres paused trying to work out if Maria was taking the awful information in and she was not too upset.

"I also think, so does your boss; you replaced the last person who tried to go public. Erin doesn't know who it is or anything, I think Erin will have to arrest you or she's going to let everything out and if she has a plan that should delay them. She is not giving them any clues, she's just following procedure. I'm not sure she knows what she's doing, she's all over the place and worried sick about you."

"I will be fine you know – I have not done anything wrong." Maria said, she hoped she was right.

"I think that's what Erin was saying I don't think it matters. Look, I have to take you to my contact and they will get us some paper. Erin said it had to be in black and white. They cannot delete the information can they?" Ceres paused, choosing to ignore her question, Maria knew the answer it was written clearly on Ceres' face she had confirmed her fears by her omission. "Come on lets go we are running out of time." Maria just followed quietly accepting her fate all the while thinking of ways of letting the public know this was wrong and she knew it. If she was going to lose her job, she was going to let the world know what they were doing. If it took, all her life she made a pact with herself she would release this information and she would not let anyone get hurt through this.

They headed towards the port; this was where Ceres' contact lived. They tried to keep out of everyone's way, trying to look as if they belonged there. It was seedy on this side of the conurbation and Maria had never been in this area in her life, her mother had been quite well off, although the area in which Maria lived was not quite as popular as it had been, she was shocked at the houses in the area where she now stood.

"I thought they'd knocked these down years ago." Maria mumbled to no one in particular. Row upon row of ancient small terraced houses and old apartment buildings the spaces so small between each building, many on the water's edge. Blackened with age the dereliction was rife, old plastic cracked boxes being used as covers for the homeless. The utopia of Maria's childhood was not blessed by all. Many lived in each house or apartment there was no privacy for anyone.

"I've told you before that the State don't look after those out off work." Ceres said having been in this area before it didn't come as a shock, her mother had lived here in her youth and this was the area Ceres had grown up.

54

Her thoughts wandered back to her childhood she tried to avoid this area at all costs. Her mother had had two or three jobs to educate her and since she had died, Ceres got upset at coming home. It had only been a year she was still raw unlike Maria who had time to get used to being alone, although she was so glad for her friend and she would do anything to help her now. The rotten smell emitted from the dock, blackened timber rotten from the heat and the crustations sucking away any beauty it once had. Those houses, Ceres would never call them homes; were over crowded only the upstairs were habitable. The floods had destroyed the lower floors of many.

Maria had never been invited back to where she lived and although she had lost her family and was always thought of as the one who needed looking after. Ceres had gone through life fighting for everything she needed. Since the war, no one had families as such, just people who they could rely on and helped. Ceres was not so lucky to have an early year's education, her mother had taught her at home and when they could afford for her to go to school, she felt inferior and not quite good enough to mix with other children until Maria befriended her.

When she met Erin who's mother had always worked and they were well off she was over awed by her constant complaining that she never saw her mother. Ceres had the same problem but had no one to turn too when she needed someone. The three of them made an odd sight, each from different backgrounds each with different problems. Ceres smiled to herself since the laws had changed and you had to earn to get by; those that had money or the experience did well but those that didn't have the money were left to their own devices, there was no equality everyone had to work -

or starve. Many complained of the men in the enclosures, a few thought that they were an inconvenience and the way they were kept, starving families could benefit from the amount of food, they were given. After all, they were only kept for their sperm.

Ceres hated theses houses, a few only lived on the first floor after the floods - the downstairs were uninhabitable.

"Does it always smell like this?" Maria questioned horrified at the accommodation.

"You get used to it after a while." Although, the smell always made Ceres nauseous. Stepping over the seaweed in the middle of the road, from the tide line, they stepped gingerly down the slippery stone steps from the barrier. Their shoes slipped on the crustaceans forming on the steps; carefully they went down to the underside of the harbour. Ceres stopped at an opening in the wall barely enclosed by the door that was held miraculously by the hinges. The grey door was chipped showing a bottle green paint underneath, where it had been battered by the sea and ever growing debris. Ceres banged on the wood; it seemed an age before anyone answered her knocking.

"Hello?" The unknown voice echoed behind the door.

"The sea's choppy tonight," Ceres said nonchalantly. Maria turned around – confused the sea was clear and there was no wind in fact it was a beautiful evening. The door creaked slowly open; inside Maria saw the walls dripping from the curved ceiling and it stunk. The damp effused her senses; a cold chill ran through her.

"Come in" half hidden behind the door was someone who obviously dressed in clothes that didn't fit her. The shirt hung off her shoulder, her greasy once strawberry blonde hair slipped down her back; her face had a slightly green cast enhanced by her sunken cheeks.

"Is Betty here?" Ceres asked.

"You'd better come in and see her Heather"

"Thanks Eustace" Maria looked askance at Ceres, "Heather?"

"Ssh" Ceres indicated her to be quiet.

"Who's your friend?" Eustace asked Ceres

"She needs help – but I'll only speak to Betty." Maria was tired – nothing as yet had sunk in, she was exhausted as she followed Ceres slowly farther and farther into the depths under the city, the stagnant smell was starting to make her wretch.

"Betty!" Ceres exclaimed giving her acquaintance a hug. Maria felt this unknown woman was her last hope – Ceres surprised her with how many people she knew Maria was oblivious as to how little she knew of Ceres' life. They had been friends forever. Erin briefly entered her head, what if – she knew about Ceres, about these people, they had always protected her. A new dawning entered into her conscious. The friends that had been her rock were virtually strangers. Although Erin seemed to know more about Ceres than she did, why did they always protect her from the big bad world? She would probably deal with this better if they had not.

Ceres was ensconced in deep conversation with this stranger, her short dark hair, slicked back like the men in the old movies Maria had watched as a child. The shirt she was wearing could do with a wash, Maria berated herself for her judgements, she didn't know this woman and it was as if she had walked into a different world.

Maria couldn't believe she felt a stab of jealously, she was not listening to what they said – she was afloat now and she didn't know where the tide was going to take her. *Just follow what they do and I will be fine. What if?* She didn't know what the outcome would be. She had no idea of what this would do to her life. She didn't care anymore – Why did she always want to be the hero? Look where this had got her. Maria slumped down on the mould-smothered floor. Exhaustion taking over, her eyelids dropped – she should have taken notice of Ceres was saying – instead everything darkened around her.

"Is she ok?" Betty abruptly interrupted the conversation.

"I think it's all getting to her," Ceres paused – "You know I don't think she knows what she's walked into."

"You realise I cannot jeopardise our organisation." Betty said – Ceres could physically see the frustration on Betty's face – this sort of corruption was what she had been waiting for, probably a gift. Ceres needed to protect Maria as far as she could.

"I think we'll let her sleep" Ceres said aloud "You know – she's going to get caught anyway – my friend will not be able to protect her for long."

"We need to keep the evidence – they'll hush it up to the pyramid, make out she's got an over active imagination. I don't think the time's right for this to come out – no-one is going to believe her." Betty mused to herself. Ceres, realising the truth, was hurt. It was going to hurt them all. "Suppose we make it look as if no one knows it, just her," Betty pointed at Maria who was oblivious to it all. She was about to be let down by her closest friends.

"Do you have an unauthorised computer here?" Ceres asked. Betty was her last hope of getting Maria away from the pyramid, she should have known Betty would not risk everyone just for a favour – Erin had already known this. Members had been left before, never mind a higher-ranking intellectual.

"Come with me – I need to download the data – I've got some paper to make a hard copy – as we discussed" Betty, stated 'Do you know how difficult it is to get that stuff now – most of my contacts have been caught – my supply's drying up.

Ceres had not seen such an archaic computer it should have been in a museum. With no talk back facility, just a keyboard, Ceres didn't know where to begin.

"I know – we found it in a skip – someone's grandmother – it's not been chipped though," Betty laughed at Ceres' scepticism her voice rose a few octaves in sarcasm; "...and with a few upgrades it is compatible old but still comparable!" "Here I'll help." Ceres didn't know where to turn it on. Moving Ceres out of the way pushing buttons she got Ceres into the space. "All yours – by my reckoning you will have an hour before your friend has to go to Maria's home, we need every trace of you and her removed from the apartment what's the code?" Betty paused, her face slightly contorted from the concentration that was ingrained within each hard worn line. "I'll get some of my operatives to go clean up the place. You then need to get Maria back to her original home. Do you think she'll cope?"

Ceres wondered if Betty ever paused for breath. She could understand why she was a good interrogator she had the ability to throw you off guard. Ceres didn't answer Betty with a direct answer she only could manage a shrug with her shoulders. She felt she was abandoning her closest friend – there was no way out.

"Ok let's get on with it – I've got to protect my tracks and protect Maria's work."

A glimmer of light could be seen on the horizon. Dusk

enveloped them – it normally would have made Ceres feel safe, there was something about this time of the day returning to the night gave her a warm feeling, this time she was holding Maria so tight as she sobbed into her friend's shirt. They had done their best – if they couldn't protect Maria, they could protect what she had found. If only Vanessa had not been so scared – they would all be safe instead they were about to give their friend to the lions.

"Come on – let's get you inside" Ceres said not knowing when she would see Maria again. "We'll be here whatever happens – don't you forget that." Tears now running down Ceres' cheeks too "Go on" she gave Maria a slight nudge toward her home.

Maria walked slowly forward each leg ached, the gravity seemed to be overactive, today pulling her further into the walkway as her home grew nearer. Ceres watched Maria walk into her block; turning her back, she lifted her arm,

"Erin Holt – monitor" her communicator glimmered into life.

"Hi – OK?" Erin appeared in front of her as a hologram.

"Done." Ceres said slightly baring her teeth – it was not Erin's fault but she could have done more. For God sake, it is all about her job, they would let Maria down. As usual, Erin was all business – Ceres cut her off the communicator without listening for Erin's reply. She felt sick, empty and guilty. Ceres lent over the flood barrier, tears trickled down her face into the sea.

Maria felt very alone in her apartment, walking slowly – picking up her mother's photograph, she had never felt so alone - *they think I am oblivious – they don't think I have any idea.* Her own voice echoed around the vast space – *What a waste, my whole life has been achieving a dream – that has already been*

60

achieved and no one wants. For the first time Maria listened to her voice – her dreams collided with the reality inside her mind. Idiocy – the question now was how long Erin could keep them away – she couldn't put off the inevitable. *However, what would that be*?

8

Erin shuffled from one foot to another, her hand kept returning to her communicator; she was waiting for Georgina outside the department for the Praeposter's.

The hovercraft waited for them ominously on the lawn. Erin wanted to turn and run, Ceres was hardly speaking to her. *It was if it was her fault*, a small voice inside reminded her that it was her cynicism that put them in this predicament.

"Hi" Erin jumped – she is never here already "I've got the order passed – she'll see the judge in the morning" Georgina called from the entrance.

"Oh, that was quick" Erin replied her voice sounding slightly too high. "I've got all the data here," Erin said quickly and lowering her voice so Georgina would not notice her lapse, holding up the data is the sultry air, so Georgina could see it clearly.

"Great, let's go – I cannot see us needing any back up – you must have known her at college" Erin's stomach did a somersault, why had she not seen this – *think!*

"Yeh – I know her – just to say hello too, of course" Erin paused wondering just how much Georgina knew, *was this a test?* "We moved in different circles." Georgina just smiled and Erin didn't know how to react.

"Come on then – I've got a party to go to this evening" Georgina said – suddenly all business.

Erin got into the hover, letting Georgina put in the co-ordinates not paying any attention to anything – dazed – not knowing who she worked for and she now couldn't remember why?

"We're here" Georgina literally bounced out of the hover. I love this part of my job. Erin could say with some certainty she didn't feel the same way.

Erin went into a sort of trance not expecting Maria to acknowledge her. The waiting for her to answer her intercom was interminable. She hoped she was OK. She had a feeling it was going to be the hardest thing she was ever likely to do. Why did it have to happen now?

Maria heard the intercom she sat as they repeated the call – she knew as she sat on her sofa Erin would have to come up and collect her - she would not let anyone else come, they would have a problem keeping her away. Maria ignored the entry system totally; she knew they could enter her apartment, without letting them in. She had heard of people disappearing before and no one heard from them again. *What would happen to her?* She didn't know. Maria was not even sure Erin knew, she had only been in the department less than 12 months. None of them knew what they had agreed; once they had left the safety of the college. Erin constantly thought of her career and Ceres was always talking about the injustice of the world they lived in, of the Praeposter's and the superpanoptican society.

Erin walked up the stairs with trepidation; she had never felt this way in her life – walking into the hallway, was comparable with walking into a stately home – Erin's memory jogged back to Maria giving them all a history lesson in her mother's apartment, now hers. Always bohemian Jane Stevenson had moulded her daughter in the same way. The institutional green paint was peeling off the walls – the old buildings couldn't compete with this climate. It never ceased to amaze her how ornate the ironwork was, they had such primitive equipment, forges and the like. She stopped on the mezzanine level wondering what a glorious building this must have been, looking down to the entrance the chandelier once so majestic hung with most of the crystal missing, leaving the green skeletal frame bare. Georgina was in a different timeframe; Erin's seemed to have slowed down. Every moment enhanced, the adrenaline pumping around her body was slowing down – time was returning to normal.

"Come on – slow coach" Georgina said smiling down to her. You know the procedure, both of us have to be here." Erin, still dazed realized how far Georgina had gotten and took the steps two at a time sweeping around to Maria's front door.

The knocking on the door seemed to reverberate around the apartment *do I answer it or not? No.* Maria knew she was putting off the inevitable. Erin stood the other side of the door wishing she could be anywhere else except here.

"Right – we're going in" Georgina pulled out a square object from her pocket.

"What's that?" Erin asked but somewhere in her distant memory she knew – her mother had one in their home and she used to play with it as a child.

"A magnetiser, useful for opening locked doors – no matter how many locks." Without a thought, she placed it on the door and placing her thumb over the plastic panel a series of red lights flickered into life. "When those go green it means the lock is opened." Georgina explained as if she were a child of five. Erin resented this and for a second she forgot what she was about to do. One by one the lights flickered from red to green Erin knew there were five locks, but she was not forthcoming with any of this information to Georgina, the longer it took the more time Maria had on her own.

Georgina made the final check on the door and then spoke into the magnetiser.

"Open" the door opened slowly, as if it knew not to let in visitors, Erin hoped it didn't log her voice on the recognition panel; thankfully, Ceres had somehow eradicated it.

"Maria Jane Stevenson – you have appropriated some information from the main database" Georgina did her speech and Erin who stood behind her knew Maria was pretending to be asleep. Her heavy breathing gave her away – normally it was only a whisper when she slept. Georgina went over to her on the settee, Erin slightly but with purpose moved her out of the way.

"Why don't you make a cup of tea?"

"That is not procedure" Georgina replied, Erin thought she had the look of a robot and was getting irritated.

"No, but I shouldn't imagine you normally find people asleep when you come to collect them, either." Erin paused – trying to sound calmer, "It'll be ok – like you said she will know who I am. We met in college, remember" Erin gently eased her out of the way toward the kitchen.

"Just make sure she doesn't run." Georgina stated.

"That's highly unlikely," Erin, said with a smile, "I am a karate champion after all, the Praeposter's department paid for it." Georgina once out of earshot in the kitchen, Erin leaned over Maria.

"Maria, don't open your eyes, don't even acknowledge me they are taking you to the security prison off the coast." Erin glanced quickly over to the kitchen still whispering continued. "Not to worry it's only going to be for one night and tomorrow you are going to the court. Once we get there, you are going to be put in a cell. I am going to see if I can come with you to the court, if not both me and Ceres will be there in the morning. They will not tell you any of this, as it will hinder them. Just remember whatever I say or do, I am trying to protect you, don't forget whatever happens. Ok pretend to wake." Erin paused, checking the kitchen again still no sign. She was counting on Georgina being noisy. "Now – I'll contact Ceres later, we will see what we can do. I also think they are testing me, they know we are friends; I don't think they know about Ceres, but I will check it out. Don't be scared. I will sort out Georgina, I know she can be overzealous at times, ignore her."

Maria opened her sapphire blue eyes, wiping away her auburn, almost brown hair from over her face and looked at Erin, her eyes were glassy trying to hold back tears; Maria knew she would not let them fall. She had always admired Erin for her strength. No words were necessary as they shared a closeness.

Erin was horrified she couldn't show it – Maria had no emotion at all it was as if someone had put a mask on her friends face, her eyes were dull. ith a small nod she glanced at the kitchen. She understood. Ceres and she had underestimated her. The corner of Erin's mouth turned into a small smile. They both understood each perfectly.

"Cup of tea?" Georgina came into the room. "Have you told her - her rights?"

"No need" Erin turned to Maria "They will be no need for violence; you are going to be fine aren't you." It was neither a question nor an order, merely a statement. Maria opened her mouth to speak but her voice seemed to have seized in her throat. She had to physically fight to get the words to form into a sound.

"Yes" Although hoarse – that was all Maria said.

"Good – drink that tea and you will be able to use your voice." Georgina pushed the tea toward her. The tea worked its way down her vocal cords. Erin went into her bedroom and removed Maria's walking clothes socks and shoes. It was not the rainy season, so the nights were cold and where they were taking her, so she would need some warm clothes. She also removed a sleeping bag and a thermal ground mat. *She had to be prepared.*

Overloaded, Erin walked into the lounge and dropped the items onto the floor.

"It's not the idea to make the suspect comfortable." Georgina gave Erin a slight reprimand; however, she had thought out her options.

"Oh, I'm sorry; I thought since she was staying overnight, she would need night clothes and bedding." Erin paused for effect, cultivating the innocent look that was on her face, she hoped it was not too over dramatic. "You did say it was my first arrest, I just presumed she needed them." Georgina obviously was not expecting that, so Erin pushed her luck. "Is she allowed to take toiletries, she is in court tomorrow."

"Now Erin – please don't say anything further." A bit ruffled Georgina couldn't believe anyone could be so naive. "Yes if you must, but it will be dusk soon so hurry." Erin didn't need telling twice. With a furtive eye movement towards the clothes, she went to get Maria's toiletries. Taking Erin's lead Maria realized she was trying to help. She put on all the clothes that were littering the floor. Amazed at some of the garments Georgina went to take the teacup back to the kitchen when Erin reappeared.

"We would not want to leave it a mess now would we?" The sarcasm oozed from her mouth.

Through her teeth, Erin whispered to Maria.

"Get them all on even the trousers you will need them for tomorrow. Give me your mother's ring – they will take everything of value off you once we leave. Quickly" Urgently Maria dressed and passed over her

67

ring it was a family heirloom. The platinum with a yellow diamond ring quickly became a feature on Erin's right hand. Picking up the sleeping bag and mat she nodded for Maria to follow her.

"Georgina – are you ready?" She called trying to sound light.

"Yep, I just needed the loo she shouted," Erin was not sure it that was true but smiled anyway.

"You did OK; a bit soft if you ask me – but OK." Georgina said as she walked from the apartment onto the shabby hallway. Maria followed under Erin's silent guidance, Erin surreptitiously picked up Maria's key card as she left and put it in her pocket. Maria turned to see what she was doing as Georgina was already at the entrance eager to be off, Erin just winked.

The hover journey was comfortable. Maria slept in the back all the way, exhaustion eventually taking over her body. Erin had volunteered to mind her whilst Georgina guided them to the Panopticon.

"Maria, wake up we're nearly there," Erin whispered into her ear whilst slightly shaking her. Maria woke up startled not quite knowing where she was.

"It's OK; I can see it on the horizon, here drink this" Erin passed her a drink of water, pointing toward the tower out of the window, it loomed above the hills. *God Maria would need all her senses to cope with this.* It looked eerie in the twilight, the red rays of the sun glinted off the golden brick of the tower. It looked terrifying and beautiful at the same time. Maria turned to see what Erin was looking at. Squinting against the glare of the sun, she saw the Panoptican growing ever larger as they came closer. They had both been taught about these places at school but no one had told either of them how imposing it was. Maria's shock was starting to wear off and now her body seemed to grow rigid with fear. The window at the top of the tower glinted in the light, Maria's eyes grew wide, she had the look of a wildcat that was about to pounce. Erin held her hand to calm her, feeling totally inadequate.

"Oh look, isn't it beautiful from a distance the water surrounding it seems to enhance it somehow." Georgina broke their silent contemplation. "Sorry to tell you Maria it's really a great disappointment when you are close to it."

"One night only" Erin whispered "you are going to be fine." Although she now was starting to have doubts, no one had an easy time in there. No one was cleared. Judgement had already been made – however she had no idea – as to the security level she came under, and they didn't allow her access. Although she could find out once she had been in court.

The ride over the water was slightly bumpy; the gates grew from the ground in front of them never ending. They were huge in comparison to the circle of wall that went away from each gate, which was three metres thick.

"Prisoner – Maria Jane Stevenson" Georgina spoke via her communicator to the tower.

"Holding bay 627" obviously the woman in the tower had scanned their vehicle and they were expected. The hover lurched through the gates and followed the gravel pathway around the inside of the circle of the wall. Eventually they came to a cell that was empty, the old-fashioned iron bars hidden in the depths of the inner wall. The rising damp appeared green against the brickwork marring the building. What had looked so beautiful from a distance, the closer it loomed above her, the damp and the blackened spore-ridden stonework had left hideous scars. Inside was a dirty window letting very little light into the chamber, this was the only view into the world beyond.

There was no bed of any description. Maria realized she was better off than the other inmates as Erin had packed her sleeping bag and mat; she was going to need them.

"Be safe – see you tomorrow," Erin whispered. Georgina refused to step out of the hover, apparently, rats were common in the cells. Erin passed Maria her water and a glucose bar, knowing meals were not provided. There was no way Erin could comfort Maria. Maria knew this and slowly tears came from her eyes onto the mouldy floor below.

Erin got back into the comfort of the hover, she made herself look at Maria as the bars of the holding bay 627 closed and the silhouette of her friend could clearly be seen in the cell. Before she could do anything the hover started to disappear from Maria's view, although Erin couldn't see her friend she tightly grasped Maria's ring all the way home.

Maria glanced at her new surroundings trying not to take in too much detail. Grasping the precious water and glucose bar, she huddled within her sleeping bag for comfort. Maria made a decision *this is the last time I will cry, they are not, going to take away my pride.*

9

"You have been brought into this courtroom on a very serious charge. We don't agree with your politics Stevenson." Maria stood staring at this woman – the judge. How could this creature in a gold metallic cape judge her?

"The underground movement that you are part of is a disgrace. Will you give the names of your associates?" Maria's thoughts were racing, her attention wandered around the vast room. Court clerks in a metallic blue, and the lawyer's silver. They reflected on the glass that surrounded her. Was it supposed to intimidate her? It just made her determined they were not going to beat her. She shook her head, her attention returning to what that gold woman and her she-devils were saying.

"No, ma'am."

"Very well then." The judge took a long pause. She was stood behind glass, not to mix with the other women in the room. "I will not understand why we should let the males out of the camps to let them extinguish the human race forever. We live in a truly democratic society. The problem we have today arose from greed and disorder." The judge turned her full attention onto Maria. Noticing the judge's reaction, Maria pulled herself up to her full height; the system was not going to make her into a robot. "Therefore, Maria Jane Stevenson – I charge you with dishonouring the females of the human race. Your punishment shall be to have a child of the male gender." A cry of disbelief from the gallery was heard, the judge looked sharply and returned her attention to Maria. "If you are so intent on repopulating this world with men, you shall for yourself see what heartache they can inflict." The judge smirked ever so slightly when she watched the horror dawn on the offender's face.

Maria was let out of the glass cage. Two security guards were waiting for her outside, they tried to push her in between them but she refused and walked out on her own. They took her to the institute of medical health. It smelt of metal, she could taste it as she walked through the door, she didn't know what they were going to do with her. Would there be instruments?

A large woman came towards her. When she got closer, she realized that she was a medic.

"Confirm your name."

"Maria Jane Stevenson." The computer verified she was who she said she was. The medic left her, terrified. She didn't say anything else, just walked off behind the white wall. She couldn't go far, although she was alone, the laser beams and the in-house computer would seal all entrances before she got anywhere near escaping. Her instincts were telling her to run.

She looked around the room; it was so clinical. The last time she had been in the institute was when they told her that her mother had died of a rare reaction to the chemical imbalance in the food. They were no use then even with the advance in technology. What were they going to do with her? The question repeated in her brain. The medic returned with a drink.

"Please take a drink you must be thirsty after today." Thankful for some kindness she accepted gratefully and drank it in three gulps. She started to feel woozy.

"Computer, bed please." The single bunk, slide gently out of the wall. Maria watched the room spin around her until the blackness enveloped her.

"Is she asleep yet?" The large medic asked the physician, who was standing in her evening gown.

They were watching Maria via a computer screen.

"I have to go out this evening and I don't wish to be waiting around till she decides to sleep – she is a convict after all." The physician's impatient attitude mirrored her disgust at the patient. She had known her through university.

"I think she is now under sedation. I think she must have been exhausted with the day she's had." The medic replied. "I'll go and get the frozen sperm."

Madeline looked at her patient, the girl most likely to go places in there year top of her field in biochemistry. Why she got involved with those troublemakers, she would never know. The quicker the procedure is completed, the fewer problems there will be from the judicial system. It was better that she didn't have to think of the consequences of the punishment.

"I've got it." The medic returned breaking Madeline from her thoughts. "I'm nervous about assisting with this I've never done this before."

Madeline looked at her medic and saw the apprehension in her face.

"It is a simple enough procedure. A quick insertion of a catheter into her womb, inject the semen – test the gender get that ascertained then we let nature do the rest." Maria was laid out, on a surgical table and these two people unknown to her changed her life forever.

At Maria's flat her friends consoled each other on her demise. Yet, each was secretly glad it was not either of them who was standing in the dock, and that Maria had not given their names to the authorities. Erin thought it couldn't get any worse than when she left her at Panoptican.

"I can't believe they just took her away like that, like some animal," Ceres was ranting as usual – it was her idea of dealing with a problem. She had assumed

73

they needed her guidance. She was feeling guilty it was their fault they couldn't save her.

Ceres' eyes slowly wandered around the room taking in Maria's white walls, the lighting that came through glass panels embedded in the walls and floor. It was all glass, looking out onto the sprawling city below. Her thoughts wandered back to Maria's house, and her old-fashioned eccentricities, having a sofa (was that what she had called it?). With its very odd furniture that you couldn't possibly put away, her rooms were compartmentalised for different things, not having a large space to use as one needed it. This was why Ceres liked her so much, her quirky ways. Her eyes rested on her friend's picture; she slowly picked out her features one by one. Maria's hair was thick and blonde, compared to Ceres' own mousy brown. If only her mother had changed that gene. However, wasn't that the misuse she was fighting against? She couldn't say her friend was pretty in the usual sense - handsome maybe. She wanted to laugh at herself, who didn't blame their mother for something – another gift from her mother's prejudices.

"Ceres? Are you OK?" Erin asked concerned but not giving her time to answer. "Do you think she'll be alright when she's let out of confinement, what I mean is when is it three months or four? No one will talk to her." Erin paused; she started to think of the implications to herself. Would she be excluded from work? If she were seen to be talking to such an obvious criminal? She was not going to let them down now, it was a stupid bloody idea when they were all so close. Confessions - who needs them?

Erin trying to hide her thoughts unsuccessfully rambled on. "What I mean is, the State pays for their confinement, and what is she going to do when it's time for delivery? No one has babies naturally anymore. She will die in agony. You would think they would have perfected that by now – you know that womb thing."

"I think you have said enough she will need our help, don't forget she has to have this child until he is five." Ceres paused collecting her thoughts "the one good thing is she'll be able to see him when he goes to the enclosure." She paused again the stress plainly showing on her face. "We have to get this place ready for Maria coming home; the cleaner has broken down again. I suppose we had better not see each other for a least a year from now." She looked at Erin; she realized that Maria would only have her to rely on

Erin knew Ceres was being sensible; some how she had to face Georgina.

I've found a house where they can go – she will not be able to work in Bio Tech but once he goes to the enclosure I can get her a job working in the institute as a nurse.' Giving Ceres a hug, Erin started to cry. 'Look after her – I'll have the house ready when she's had him!' Both of them started to clean the apartment, ready for their friend's arrival.

10

"Vanessa" a smart young woman looked across her workstation; her colleague didn't seem herself lately. "Are you okay?" Rebecca asked concerned she was staring into space. She was used to her constantly wittering on about her daughter or telling her off for not getting the work done. "Sorry, yes, I am fine just thinking about things" Vanessa answered. "Work related?" Rebecca asked. "Can I help; I know how sometimes the mechanical issues can become a problem." She said. "No it's nothing to do with work it's a personal problem." Vanessa answered vaguely. "Is Natasha alright?" Rebecca asked concerned. "Oh yes, she is fine doing really well at school, she was telling me yesterday on the beach about what they are doing at the moment." Vanessa paused surveying Rebecca in front of her wondering if she classed her as a friend – she had very few since having Natasha, as she didn't join in the social side, her 'friends' still understood her daughter was now her life. "Can I ask your advice?" She asked her colleague. "Of course, God, I see more of you than I do my own Mother." Rebecca laughed she wanted Vanessa back and whatever was bothering her it couldn't be that bad.

"I had a visit a few days ago from a group of women, one was a biologist." Vanessa paused, not sure if she was doing the right thing, but she needed to talk to someone about it. "Anyway you know this genetic thing they keep saying they are looking for a correction on the news comm." She paused now she had said it allowed she actually didn't think it was so bad. "Well to cut a long story short," she said, "I was the anomaly." Rebecca had no idea what she was talking about." "Which is? This sounds confusing."

"It is the gene they were looking for, they said I have the ability to conceive a male gender naturally" she paused "therefore, I carry the anomaly, the genes to put it all right."

"Was it a practical joke you have heard Vanessa?" Rebecca asked thinking it was an impossibility. It was as if she had said she could see ghosts. "I didn't know so I repeated it to the Pyramid." Vanessa paused "They said they would investigate it. "There you go, these people aren't right in the head – I would not let it worry you." Rebecca stated.

"You don't understand, these women they were the real deal and I saw on the news comm that she had been arrested on some weird charge. I think she was telling the truth." "Seriously?" Rebecca asked, wondering if stress had made Vanessa slightly mad.

"Who did you speak to at the Pyramid?" Rebecca asked. "Georgina – she seemed a bit slap dash to be honest." Vanessa stated.

"You think about it – it is a possibility, how would we know what they have found, you daren't say a word to anyone in the Pyramid." Vanessa said. "Do you really think that?" "Yes, I am thinking of going to news comm, I think it's true." Vanessa said. "So what you are telling me is that you think you are the missing link." Rebecca looked at her incredulously, "I never thought your ego was that big!" She laughed. "No I think I am one of many – how would we know?" Vanessa replied still seriously.

"Okay how about I call this Georgina and find out what she thinks before you do anything stupid." Rebecca said, "If you must, but I think we are being manipulated by them – I am going home if I hear nothing from you I will ring the news comm tomorrow – the whole thing smells of something nasty." Rebecca was perplexed she had never known Vanessa do anything rash in her life, a party girl maybe in her time, but since her daughter – never. She didn't even say goodbye she watched her colleague walk out of the building.

"Get me Georgina at the Pyramid" Rebecca stated to her computer. "Yes how can I help?" Georgina appeared before her. "My friend has an issue and has ideas about herself that may seem strange, but she is saying that you are investigating it." "What is that?" Georgina asked and who is your friend?" "Her name is Vanessa Gresval and she spoke to you a few days ago." "Yes I remember" Georgina wondered where this was heading. "Well she was saying" Rebecca could not quite believe she was saying this, "she has said she is the cure for the human race and it is being covered up as she has heard nothing from yourselves."

Rebecca finished with a sigh. "Really?" I cannot imagine why. "I will contact her today, is she at home or at work?" Georgina asked. "Home" Rebecca answered. "Please don't mention this to anyone else, as I am sure you know it is all a little far-fetched." Georgina said. "I thought so; I thought I would ask though." Rebecca shrugged it was not anything to do with her, all seemed odd though.

Georgina sat in her office pondering over what was said. If she took this to Erin she would take the credit; as she did with the arrest of that stupid biologist. This time she would deal with it herself. This couldn't get out there, there would be riots and anyone working for the Pyramid would be slain. All these men, and the women who bore them, would be after blood goodness knows what would happen to them they would be hung, drawn and quartered.

What if Vanessa went to the news comm.? There was only a certain amount of coverage they could control without people getting suspicious. She had two options; neither had she had the stomach for. Neither boded well for this Vanessa Gresval, but Georgina thought she should learn to keep her mouth shut.

"I need to contact the 'incarceration team'". Georgina stated into her office computer.

"It is done, do you wish to speak to anyone in particular" the monotonous tone of the computer reverberated around the room.

"No, anyone will do it is urgent" Georgina said.

"Hello how can I help?" A woman in a nurse's outfit appeared before her.

"Yes we have a problem". Georgina stated.

"Explain further please"

"We have a leak that needs to be plugged." Georgina laughs at her own joke. "Seriously, Vanessa Gresval is causing difficulties, she has been discussing the human genome has rectified itself."

"Fancy that." The woman obviously knew the truth. "We cannot have that now can we?"

"My thoughts exactly." Georgina stated.

"Can you rectify this situation please?" "That will not be a problem."

"Are there any complications?" The institutionalised woman asked.

"One, she has a daughter – we thought it was not an issue once we found out she had the anomaly we gave her a promotion – I have checked her file – we obviously were not careful enough." Georgina said with regret.

"So be it, that poor girl – she will be safe, I will put her in one of our best homes."

"Thank you for that, please let me know when the sorry business is complete." Georgina hated this part of the job, she only joined the Pyramid for the kudos and parties. She found it distasteful.

"Vanessa Gresval" a voice came through the door communicator. "Yes?" Vanessa answered.

"Can we have a word please? We have come to discuss the interview you had at the Pyramid."

"Of course come up". At last, Vanessa was pleased someone was taking her seriously. Two women came into her apartment, both in black and very formal in appearance; Vanessa found this comforting.

"Can I get you a drink?" Vanessa asked.

"No, we are fine." The smaller woman spoke. "We have just come for a chat really."

"No problem what would you like to know?" Vanessa said sitting down.

"Could you please explain your thoughts on the visitation the other evening?"

"Of course, where would you like me to start?" Vanessa asked.

"Any way you wish to." The small woman answered, Vanessa thought the other lady must be a mute.

"Obviously you know what I have said previously to Georgina." Vanessa said. They both nodded. "I have had a thought on what those women were saying, they may well have been on to something. I'm not saying I'm special or anything, but this anomaly in the genome, it could be true after all. How would we know, we are all inseminated under controlled conditions. What if I actually had sex with someone, could I have permission to meet one of the men in the enclosures?" She laughed at herself. "I wouldn't know what to do; I would have to look at the old pictures to see what they did. Is it like sleeping with a woman? I'm sorry I'm digressing." Vanessa could see they thought she had lost it, but it had to be said. "Anyway what was I thinking, how do we know what is the truth and what has lead us to false information?"

"I see you have had a stressful week" The women seemed to take pity on her.

"Yes and my daughter will be home from school soon, she is the wonder of my life."

"You have a daughter?" The small woman asked.

"Oh yes, Natasha, very bright I am very proud of her." Vanessa said smiling.

"We could give you something for the stress – only if you wish."

"That would be nice, I feel very strung out it's all very odd."

"Let my colleague give you a little something." The larger woman rummaged through her bag and pulled out a small pot from which she retrieved two pills and handed them to Vanessa who promptly took them.

"Oh these are good. I feel very chilled." Vanessa said, the room suddenly blurred, if she had been compos mentis she would have been worried, as it was she went to sleep where she sat.

The larger woman stood up and checked her pulse.

"I will take her now."

"I shall wait for her daughter here, and then send her to her new home." She paused "Are you informing the Pyramid, so they can sell her property and put it in a trust for her daughter. This one will not see the outside world ever again."

Making herself comfortable, she sat and waited for Natasha to return home. Vanessa was slung in a firefighter's lift over the shoulder of the larger woman.

"Right, I will see you tomorrow then, this one will be out for a while. When she wakes I will inject her with something nice." She said laughing.

"Mummy" Natasha came running into the apartment stopping abruptly and staring at the strange lady sitting there. "Who are you?" She said.

"I am sorry but your Mummy has been taken ill."

Natasha started to cry uncontrollably. "Come on, we will get your things. I will take you somewhere safe until she gets better." As an afterthought, she asked, "Do you have a Grandmother?"

"No" Natasha answered, still sobbing.

"Oh well" the woman smiled. "Where I am taking you is nice, there are other girls and lots of toys to play with." Natasha was not convinced.

"I want to see my Mummy."

"You will next week; she will be a bit better by then. Don't worry it will be fine."

"I don't think so." Natasha looked up confused. "I will see my Mummy, won't I?"

"Yes dear, but she is very ill and may say some odd things."

"But she will be there to give me a cuddle?"

"Of course dear, don't worry; it will all work out fine." The strange woman consoled her with lies.

"Okay then." Natasha took her hand and walked into the unknown.

11

Maria sat down exhausted, trying to collect her thoughts – the nine months were nearly over, it would not end there. Since she had returned to her home from the confinement at the institute, she had been treated like a leper. Outcast by the people she had known all her life. No one had asked what she had done to receive this thing stuck out in front of her she looked odd anyway. Last month she had contacted Ceres to come over. In a panic – she had thought she was dying. Luckily, Ceres had found some old texts at the local museum about 'pregnancy'. Apparently, the skin was supposed to stretch – not normal at all.

Maria thought her stomach was splitting open, the marks had left gashes of red splitting her stomach into lines. The thing she had a problem with most was constantly feeling sick. Luckily, that had worn off after three months, just as she was able to come home. Never would she understand these women who had this primeval urge to go through this, the lottery was evil – it was just awful – the hormone levels up and down, you never knew how you were going to react to anything – she could understand perfectly now why it was a punishment.

The baby kicked her in the ribs making her high-energy fruit juice spill (as she had it resting on top of her stomach) it interrupted her thoughts. Again, that queasy feeling started as the thought of another thing inside her, it made her want to vomit, when it's foot stuck out at the side. It reminded her of those awful alien films she had watched in the media history classes at school. This just was not a natural act at all!

"Hi." It was Ceres doing her daily check of her

friend. They both knew she could get in contact via the communicator, it was not as if she couldn't see her or anything but Ceres felt she should be there personally. "How are you feeling today?"

"Oh you know, tired fed up and wishing it was all over" Maria paused, lately she felt that every word she said was an effort. A small ironic chuckle let slip from somewhere inside she was not quite sure where.

"What are you laughing at?" Ceres asked concerned for her friend, unsure if she had gone quietly mad without her noticing – she had been under a lot of strain lately.

"I was just thinking about Amy, do you remember her from school? You know I was walking in the centre today heading for my check up at the institute."

"I didn't know you had to be regulated today, you never said." Ceres said ignoring her first statement completely.

"Oh, I must have forgotten I'm doing that a lot lately; it must be all these hormones that they insist I've got, although personally I'm not sure! Anyway, Amy, she nearly died when she saw me I think she thought I had been pumped up with something. Do you know this is what I have wanted to change for our bodies not to be tampered with?" Ceres looked at her friend now convinced she had lost the plot, unfortunately Maria caught the look "you needn't look at me that way, I know exactly what I am saying all that propaganda that is posted everywhere, to stop 'them' tampering with our bodies. I will tell you something I would not mind some tampering now.''

Maria was just slightly afraid of what was going to happen when it was time for the labour. She had heard loads of horror stories about the labour, Ceres and her had read the old books she had found and it sounded barbaric. If she had not been given this as a punishment

– she would have been able to have a stun in her back, apparently it stopped the pain. Alternatively, be unconscious throughout the procedure.

Those awful women at the institute would not even consider telling her it was something to do with the law. Why did she have to have this naturally – they said she was allowed some types of pain relief but that was all they would give her. She remembered the words of the midwife (such an old-fashioned term – some kind of custom in the medical profession). "It would not be a punishment dear as we gave you all of the medication that you ask for." She had even said it with an inane smile.

"Are you all right?" Ceres asked her full of concern.

"Yeah – I'm fine just thinking about next week," she said it was due around the 19th. "Half of me wishes it was over and the other half of me hopes this will never arrive." She looked out onto the city, "what I am feeling at the moment is totally irrational I know – so don't start telling me not to think about it." Maria paused she knew she should resent this baby, but she loved him for all she hated what it was doing to her body.

"I wasn't going too," Ceres said indignantly.

"Yes you were, I can't not think about it," she paused gasping for a breath, "it's here stuck out in front of me" she patted her stomach a bit too roughly. "It's like one of those old fashioned hot air balloons, and the pain I thought it was going to be emotionally hard, not on your life – what she meant was physical pain and I haven't even got to the best part yet!"

"Have you finished – you are ranting like a lunatic – totally self obsessed and devoid of rational thought." Ceres had listened to these outbursts since the day she came out of the institution and knew if she didn't head it off soon, she will be the main contender for torrent of abuse.

"Why don't you have an early night, relax, while you have the chance. I spoke to my friend about it all and she advised lots of rest, as you would be exhausted when it arrives. Let us be truthful my friend had help from the institute but you are not going to get any. So come on let's get you to sleep." Maria's mood had calmed down a lot and it was easier to be guided by Ceres than continue to argue.

After getting her to bed, Ceres collapsed on Maria's sofa. She had been more hysterical than usual; it must be getting near to the time. Ceres worried for her friend and was too exhausted to muster up enough energy to go home, she fell asleep on the sofa.

"Ceres!" Maria screamed from her bed, "Ceres!"

"What, what's the matter?" Ceres said stumbling into her bed area. "Are you OK?" She was still rubbing her eyes.

"I…I… Oh god, look at this!" Maria pointed to her wet sheets. "What the hell is happening?" Maria was hysterical, totally losing control with fear. Ceres pulling herself together realising that anything she said to Maria would be ignored or worse she would over react, she did the first thing that came to mind that would shock her into sense. She slapped her face.

"What did you do that for?" Maria said rubbing her flaming red left cheek.

"Trying to calm you down, that's what for. Are you in pain?"

"Oh no" Maria said sheepishly.

"Good." Ceres by now was pulling her friend out of bed and was fetching her clean clothes to change into. "Here put these on, and go and get yourself cleaned up. Then we'll examine this mess." Maria wandered off to get herself dressed, returning a lot calmer.

"I'm sorry it looks like I over reacted again, just

slightly though!" She said with a smirk. Ceres was busy hunting through the information she had down loaded onto her computer.

"Here, look at this, it seems your waters have broken. Are you sure you feel OK?"

"Yes I feel fine" Maria answered still none the wiser. "I really would love a fruit juice. Would you?"

"Now we know what's up with you, do you think it would be a good idea to call the institute?" Ceres paused; you could nearly see her brain ticking over "No, I think we will wait. Computer can you get rid of that mess in the bedroom, thank you." With that two round drones on wheels appeared from a cupboard, started to pull off the bedding and then promptly replaced it, as silently as they had come, they left. "Have you ever thought of updating your home computer? It is very dated you know." Ceres didn't say to any one in particular just observing Maria's cleaners, which were archaic. She would concede that they were cute more like pets than cleaning utensils.

"How are you feeling?" Her thoughts turning back to Maria, according to her information she should soon be starting the first stages of labour. If Maria would read it too, she would know, but as always she is too stubborn working on the principle that what she does not know will not hurt her. She also had a feeling that it was not going to be an easy night.

"I'm fine, why do you ask? Is there something I should know?" Maria felt on top of the world, her energy levels had not been this good for ages. She was also safe in the knowledge the thing inside her was not due until next week because that was what the institute had told her. Ceres just sat like a cat waiting to pounce, waiting, waiting, and waiting.

"Holy shi…!!!" Ceres pounced. Maria curled up in agony; her stomach felt like two clawed hands had just gone inside her and pulled her apart. The cramping pain eased off after a couple of minutes giving Maria enough time to grab a breath. Ceres was running around collecting things they would need at the institute as she heard another blood-curdling wail from the sofa.

"Communicator, the institute now!" Ceres now worried for her friend she had never seen anything like this sort of agony in her life. What sort of barbarians would let women go through this kind of agony? "My name is Ceres Zanuti. I am a friend of Maria Jane Stevenson. Her labour has come a week early, not next week as she was told; is this normal?"

"Unfortunately Zanuti, one cannot determine when one will give birth, as yet anyway." Ceres hated talking to computerised receptionists. They were just so clinical. "Bring her in from the way she looks there is no rush for her to be here soon."

"Are they sending the hover carrier to collect me?"

"No I'll take you in; you will be more comfortable, instead of being on the cold steel of the carrier"

"Are you sure" Maria would just prefer to go to the institute.

"Yep I'm sure, you will be fine"

"Sure?"

"Sure, positive, absolutely certain." Ceres said laughing. "Come on the let's get you sorted out."

It only took them five minutes to get to the institute, via the personal hover; the usual rush that Ceres encountered was not there as it was just past lunch. The pains were still ten minutes apart, so there was no need to rush although Maria was starting to panic.

"What was I thinking of? I must be bloody insane, I thought... Oh god, I thought." The pain came again it was agonising felt as if someone had stabbed her in the stomach. Maria paused, thinking of herself and what pain she was in. No one gave a shit whether she was here or not everyone expects her to be in bloody pain and that bloody midwife or whatever she is called. She is a tyrant. Cow, I wish that silly bitch would fall from something very, very high.

"Is Ceres allowed in?"

"You are supposed to go through this yourself. I have said before this is supposed to be a punishment you know this, young woman, why do you ask? Do you really want someone to see you like this?" The midwife answered her like she was speaking to a child.

"Look, I don't care who, what, or where I am at this present moment in time. Therefore, why should I care whether a close friend of mine sees me in this bloody institute, with it is oh so sterile walls and it is oh so friendly personnel. So why don't you trot off like a good little girl, go, and get Ceres, I didn't." Now Maria's temperament and patience was not all it could be and not at all like her usual easy going self.

"Sorry for pausing, I am in a slight amount of pain, where was I ah yes… didn't give care about the rules when I was put in this position so run along and find Ceres!" The midwife stunned by her attitude ran out of the room, she thought she might be over reacting to the pain. Although she had never seen any woman go through labour naturally before, she heard horror stories by the old midwives but the practice of late had been in disuse manly due to the enclosures being at capacity in recent years.

"How are you? Oh my God, they said you were in a bad way but this?" Ceres walked in to find Maria curled up in the corner snarling with pain. The midwife was hovering so she could check her cervix for dilation, she herself was nervous as she was going to have to rely on the computer to tell her what to do next.

"Is it possible you will be able to calm her?" the

midwife asked slightly pleading, Ceres turned around to see her friend pacing up and down as if she were a caged animal.

"Maria do you want to hold my hand?" Ceres asked tentatively.

"Please" fear pulsated through both of them.

"I feel like I am dying" Maria gasped gripping Ceres' hand tighter. "I can't do this."

The pain was now near enough constant, it was also getting worse, she had never known pain like it, the pain was unbearable – to think women not one hundred years ago still gave birth naturally, what were they barbarians? She was now at the point that she didn't have a clue how long she had been there, time was not the issue she couldn't remember not being in pain. The room started to spin, and then it went black.

"Will she be OK?" Ceres was panicking now; her friend lay unconscious on the metallic floor oblivious to the medics swarming around her. "Will she die?"

"No, she'll be fine" the medic assured her.

"What's happening to her, Maria's normally so strong, she doesn't just give up like this."

"Don't worry Zanuti, your friend has collapsed through exhaustion, it's a very tiring business giving birth, she'll be fine in a minute, just wait and see." The medic then passed over Maria's body a small hand held laser, Ceres didn't have a clue what it was, she didn't care, all she wanted was her friend back. She turned her back on her friend and the midwives and medics, not wanting to show her weakness to the others, it wasn't done. Ceres spun around as she heard a faint murmur coming from the bed.

"Maria, Maria!" Ceres said, stroking her friend's hand. Maria turned to look at her, blinking, a small smile formed on her lips. Then her face twisted and crumpled in agony.

possible.

"Great, how is she mentally?" Erin asked concerned.

"Not good – is the house ready?"

"Yes – ready and waiting – I'll meet you there as agreed." Erin and Ceres both felt protective over them.

"Do you know something – this little boy doesn't just have one parent but three." Ceres smiled.

"See you soon." The communication cut out, but Erin sat, a warm feeling came over her – she had missed them and nothing would separate her again.

Part Two

Phillip

12

"Phillip, you've got a visitor."

"Sorry?" Phillip replied trying to wake up – rubbing his eyes.

"I said you've got a visitor," the guard said. "This one looks horny, she is particularly asking for you!" She said her eyes passing over every inch of his body.

"Oh shit I'm tired can't you give her to someone else – I will make it up to you later' he said hopefully with a cheeky grin. You know I've always had a thing about women in uniform"

"I'd love to take you up on that offer, not this time I'm afraid this one's a bureaucrat." The guard replied with a look of regret fleetingly passing over her face.

"Fuck!"

"No – that's what she wants to do to you!" The guard laughed as he pulled himself out of bed he pulled on his cotton pants and strode out after her.

"Which room am I in?"

"F2" She replied

"Oh god, an even number? – I would hurry to perform to one's audience" Phillip bowed to the guard with an ironic smile stamped on his face "See you later!" He walked along the sparse clinically white corridor. He hated the non-slip stainless steel floor as always ice cold. Phillip checked the door numbers as he went past A3, B4, and B99… and so on. He thought as he wandered down the corridor it was always never ending. At last F2.

He stood outside to compose himself. It was supposed to get easier as time went by – it didn't. He found he went numb inside every time. As always, he waited outside until he was sufficiently void of emotion. With a deep breath, he opened the door he knew as soon as he stepped through it. The chip inserted into his thigh would activate the door lock. He passed through the trackers and the door bolted automatically behind him. Phillip scanned the room – not too bad he had not been in this one before. It didn't look very different to the corridor outside except for the cameras. It was better than some of the rooms he had already encountered; Phillip knew some of the other guy's preferred those rooms. He laughed at himself; he was getting quite a pro now. It had only been a couple of months.

The door opened in the corner on the other side of the room. A petite, dark-haired woman came into the room – powerful yes, he could tell the way she held herself. Pretty, he might enjoy this one; she was not much older than him. He suddenly noticed a hard glint in her eye, it made him wary.

"I thought you might be prettier." She stated

"Have you heard of me?" Phillip asked not knowing whether to be flattered or not.

"Yes, a colleague of mine, was whispering about you to her friend,"

She purred his gut was telling him something was very wrong. "Oh really, I might remember her." Phillip started to sweat he didn't like this – his blood ran cold thinking about it – something was not right.

"Erin was discussing you with a friend from way back; petite, blonde hair and blue eyes – I've never seen her before. Well what's a girl supposed to do but listen?" she smiled.

"Sorry," Phillip paused, thinking fast. "I thought you were talking to her."

"Don't be silly darling," Natasha ran her long fingernail softly down Phillip's bare chest. He felt sick wanting to know more without alarming her. It was going to be difficult. How was his mother so indiscrete,

97

she was never that lax in her judgement, especially as it was Natasha.

"So I listened in for a while after they'd got my interest in you I just couldn't wait to find out what the fuss was about. Anyway, they got onto old times; I think they were university pals. I only had one evening to wait – and look what I found – a man just coming up to his peak – muscular" Phillip sighed with relief Natasha took it the wrong way.

"Well, you are no use to me with those on" she purred pulling the Elastic of his slacks. "Get them off!" she commanded her manner changing instantly. "I didn't come here just to ramble – you know." Phillip sighed back to work. This one wanted every ounce of flesh.

"Please stand still!" The guard said. The laser washed over his body – checking for any sexually transmitted diseases easily rectified but the institute liked to keep the men clean, it was bad business sense to give the clients a disease. The shower switched on automatically, trickled over Phillips naked body. The guard was busy examining the results with the computer.

"How did you get on with Natasha?" Phillip looked up.

"I didn't realise you knew her."

"Oh yes, quite a regular – I have just emailed the footage over to her personal computer, you wouldn't believe how many that one's collected over the years." Phillip shuddered to think he was part of a collection.

"You better hurry you have to give your donation in half an hour" Phillip finished washing his body.

"Dryer" he said, warm air blasted his body from all sides.

"The computer has given you the OK – so when you

are ready you'd better get down the lab." The guard laughed 'All those girls you've fathered – Oh is it ok for me to pop by later?" She smiled "You did promise after all." Phillip laughed; he didn't mind the guards they treat him like a human being. He had heard about the other enclosures demanding sex, he shuddered.

Phillip pulled a new set of clothes from the shelves each piled neatly into compartments of different clothing: trousers, t-shirts, knickers, socks, shoes all dependant on size. He slipped on his clothes easily. Part of the wall opened revealing itself to be a door. He walked past all the doors with numbers on them towards the lab. He was already late and didn't wish to be punished by the monitor in charge of the lab. She could be a real bitch when the mood took her. His mind whirled as he hurried, wondering if that demanding cow Natasha, knew more than she was letting on. What was his mother thinking of talking about him in public it was stupid, all those years of hiding she had a son just to be reunited within the community. He would have to speak to her soon – who was this Erin she was talking about? Very odd. He turned to find a queue of men none over thirty-five.

As far as Phillip was concerned, they were the lucky ones; allowed to stay in other buildings on the complex, although very few made it above twenty-five, Phillip shivered with fear, he didn't want to die even with the life he had; this was better than none at all. Rumours were abound of men disappearing once their sperm had been reduced. The old guys lived far apart from them, he knew they had visitors normally those that work in the Pyramid. They protected their favourites he had heard in some cases the women paid for their food etc. The only woman he trusted was his mother, she was always there for him. Although naive, he never told her about the visitors it would tear her apart.

"You're an early riser," Todd said "must have been important for the guards to let them spoil their breakfast, it isn't healthy you know, not having breakfast." Todd laughed at the constant barrage of healthy specimens that they were. The institute liked healthy specimens – or was it the women?

"Yeah" replied Phillip, "you might have heard of her before – Natasha?" The men in the queue laughed.

"A real regular that one" one of the men started to smile.

"Did she get you on disk?" Todd asked seriously.

"Apparently so – Why?" Phillip was getting nervous, not only did she talk about him but now the other guy's seemed to know of her too.

"God, have you never heard of her before – you will be the talk of the dinner party set. Call it the side-show." Todd spoke quietly so as not to let the others hear their conversation. "When she has finished the meal, she shows the whole thing to her friends. Apparently, she sells them too. Publicity stunt so as to get them to come here." He paused, catching his breath. "They pay you know. That's why she's got so far up the ladder of power so quick." He laughed, "You will be inundated with requests now better keep busy down the Gym – keep up that stamina!" Todd paused a look of distaste crossed his face. "She advises which ones she enjoys, although they say she never goes back to the same man twice."

"Thank you I'm knackered thinking about it" Todd and Phillip both doubled up with laughter neither really bothered about politics nothing changed.

"X1250246" the medic barked, *here goes* Phillip thought. "Usual routine, use the booth" the medic dressed in sterilised clothing handed him a card. Phillip took the card and entered the booth with a green light flashing on the door. Phillip entered a stark cubicle he inserted his card into the slot.

"Hello   X1250246"   a   computerised   voice acknowledged him "what would you like today: previous exploits, personal strangers, classics or paper pamphlets?" Phillip suddenly realized he could watch Natasha and replay their conversation. He smiled.

"Previous exploits – Personal."

"Which?"

"Natasha" Phillip replied. The wall in front of him flashed into life with his details:

Number: X1250246

Birth Name: Phillip Richard Stevenson

Age: 18 years, 4 months, 4 days

Date of Birth: 16:04:2502

Mother: Maria Jane Stevenson

Crime: Conspiracy against the State

"Please confirm" the unanimated voice asked.

"Yes – Phillip Stevenson" Phillip answered.

"Number please – answer does not compute" Phillip laughed it was petty he knew but occasionally he enjoyed it.

"X1250246" Phillip replied. Out of the wall, a compartment opened Phillip lifted out the tube and sat down on the bench. He played with the tube between his fingers or rather the sperm suction displacer. On screen, he saw himself walk into the room F2. He smiled to himself as usual the look of complete boredom had not been erased from his face. Natasha entered, his mind drifted slightly as he watched he noticed how she looked at him with greed. It made him feel sick. What was it she said? She worked with Erin – How did she know his mother. He watched Natasha command him to take off his clothes. Did she know anything else or was she just making chit chat, some women of the women did. He knew many secrets on different bureaucrats, as many of the men did. Well whom would they talk to? Phillip's mind was playing games with him. He had too much time to think – that was all he did in here. Realising that if he didn't give a specimen there would be questions. He concentrated on the job in hand – literally.

13

Maria checked herself and her clothes over before sitting down, the waiting was horrendous. She smiled she lived for these visits. Even now after all these years, she could always see changes in her son. It was the little things, his hair may have grown the blonde curls touching his collar, he was more muscular by the day, smiling at the thought of seeing him again she just wished to give him a big hug. She wished they could go back in time to when he was hers, not part of the state inventory.

"Mama" a little boy ran across the field. He carried a small bunch of grapes in his hand.

"Yes my love." Maria was cutting their new flowers for the house, from the over abundant bushes in her garden.

"Mama, look" the small child held out a small bunch of ripened grapes to show her.

"The grapes are ready". Philip paused deep in thought "can I eat one?" He asked wide-eyed bouncing from one foot to another with excitement. Taking them from his hand, Maria pretended to examine the ripened black grapes, raising her eyebrow with a badly hidden smirk on her face.

She nodded slowly. "Aren't you a clever boy – come on, let's go and wash them." Maria stooped down looking at her son the grapes still in hand she gave him an unexpected hug. The smell of his hair wafted up her nose, tickling her face as she held him close.

"Mama, the grapes?" A muffled small voice said laughing, Maria ruffled his hair. "Come on, let's get them washed and then we can get a basket to collect some more." Grabbing his hand gently, they walked slowly up to the house.

Maria picked a bowl out of the cupboard, placing the grapes still on the vine inside it. Philip tugged at his mother's slacks. 'Mama', Maria squatted down to his height "yes my gorgeous little boy" she said in all seriousness.

"Can I help wash the grapes?" then his small face lit up with a smile, "then can we go pick some more?" "Of course my love we have to have something to munch on later." She said picking up the bowl and they both sat on the floor picking grapes off the vine Philip had brought for his Mother.

Maria stood up picking up the bowl and putting it under the running water the droplets glistened in the sink, draining it off she passed Philip the bowl. "You picked them" she grinned at him, as his face was full of excitement. "You get to eat the first one." His small hand grabbed one and he put it in his mouth savouring the sweetness. "Come and grab a few and we'll go and pick some more." Bouncing he grabbed a few and put some in his pocket for good measure. "Come on sweetheart lets go down to the vineyard."

Slowly they walked down the hill the sun glistened off the distant shores, Philip ran ahead.

"Come on Mama." He popped another grape into his mouth "The sun will set before we get there". "All in good time sweetheart". Maria savoured each moment with her beautiful little boy.

"Have you been waiting long?" A strange woman with short hair, and tattoos on her arms broke into her memory. "No not long, I like to get here early to spend as much time as I can with my son". Maria answered. "I know, I miss my little boy so much my heart brakes each time I go home". She smiled. Maria was shocked she didn't seem the type to miss anyone. She checked herself mentally, she should not judge anyone, and she knew the stomach churning feeling as the time ticked by each moment precious, for anyone. "It will soon fill up" the woman said, "I hate this bit, wish they could let us go and see them straight away.

Maria nodded in agreement, trying not to get impatient. "How old is your son?" Maria asked she had to make conversation when she really didn't wish to. She was happy with her own treasured memories and wanted to return to them it was her way of coping. She thought of the good times not sitting in a waiting room because someone deemed it normal – it was not.

"He's 25 now," she said, full of pride. "He has grown into a beautiful man, but he's still my baby". A smile broke over her harsh lined face. "How old is your son?" "Just turned eighteen," Maria said, "my baby has become an adult" she said there was no smile on Maria's face.

"The poor boy, I hope he copes with it all". The large woman shook her head. "I am sorry; I wish I could do something about what happens here, who would listen to people like us?" Physically shaking herself and gently patting Maria's arm "Hey love, he will be fine – sometimes I think they are safer in here than out there with us. "Thank you" was all she said, she knew she was well intentioned and the sentiment was properly felt.

"Oh, here is someone else – wonder if she has heard when we can go and see them" Another mother walked into the sparsely decorated room. "Hey love" the lady called over to the dishevelled, slightly haunted woman who had joined them. "You heard when we can see them?"

"No, they never tell you anything here" she shook

her head. Maria was hardly listening to them, she just waited; they had got into a deep conversation and Maria had no idea what they were talking about. She stared at the wall in front of her, it was not a grey wall she was seeing – she was in her vineyard with her little boy.

"Mama look, see" Philip stood pointing at the ripened grapes.

"Aren't you a clever boy." Maria said "Come on lets go and pick some, then we can eat them later". She picked up the basked that was lying on the parched grass, I'll pick them at the top and you pick them at the bottom." Maria carefully cut the grapes with secateurs and placed them in the basket. Philip picked some at the bottom putting some in the basket then popping one in his mouth each time. "You will be sick," Maria said.

"Mmmm" Philip said unconvinced "they are nice Mama".

"I know sweetheart, but leave some room for dinner," Maria said watching him as he intently concentrated on picking the ripened grapes. Placing her secateurs on the floor as she quickly picked up her Philip to give him a big hug, his legs dangled as she kissed his face.

"Mama" she laughed as she placed him down on the ground like a precious breakable object. Laughing, she tickled him until he giggled trying to wriggle away from her he scampered off and she ran after him.

"I am coming to get you" she called.

"You have to catch me first" he called back, running in and out of the vines. Laughing and slightly winded she caught up with him. "Ha Ha" she said laughing, "I got you" swinging him round in the air kissing him as she did so. His laughter echoed around them, in contrast to the peaceful setting and serenity of the place. Tackling him to the floor, they both laughed and both were winded as they lay on the parched grass. Holding his hands, they both looked into the sky looking at the fluffy clouds meandering across it.

"Look mummy, a rabbit with a fluffy tail" Philip said pointing at the cloud. "I see it" she said "are there anymore we can see?"

"Maria Stevenson" a harsh voice interrupted her thoughts.

"Yes" she replied standing up focusing on where the voice emanated from. "Come this way" the guard stated "good luck and enjoy your time" the lady said next to her. "Hopefully they will call me soon".

Maria followed the guard through the open doorway, the bright lights slightly blinded her for a moment – it reminded her of the day in the vineyard. Excitement welled up inside her, they walked slowly and to what seemed to be an eternity into what was an immaculately groomed garden. Benches were dotted around far enough away from each other to ensure some privacy.

He was sitting bolt upright, at one of the tables in the distance; she smiled 'their bench' she muttered.

"I'm sorry, did you say something?" the guard asked. "No, I just spoke out loud". That had been 'their bench' since the first visit to this awful place; they chose it together where she wanted him to herself. She was able to give him a cuddle and he could cry with no one else to see. She could recognise the outline of him anywhere as it was embedded in her mind. "I will leave you now," the guard stated. Maria watched her turn and walk away to collect another 'boy' to see his mother. Making sure she was not coming back and losing her dignity, she ran over to her son and didn't care if anyone saw her.

Running up she caught him from behind in a massive hug and she kissed the top of his mop of curly blonde hair. "Ouch! He involuntary said, wincing from the pain, but soon collecting himself he grinned, stood up, and returned the hug. She had to look up at him nowadays, love washed over her as she hugged him; it was as if he was three again for a brief moment. "Oh sweetheart, what has happened" horror washed over her as she held her son at arm's length examining his face. "Nothing Mama" he said, "I hurt myself in the gym – I was stupid". A look of disbelief crossed her face; she gently stroked the side of his cheek.

"I will be fine," he said trying to put her mind at ease. "Come tell me what has been going on – nothing much has happened here, all very boring." He lied as best he could. Maria knew he was lying, but didn't wish to bring up the subject as she now had firsthand experience of what her precious son was used for. It made her feel sick they both knew they were holding something back, but the subject was not broached between them. Today was there day and 'their bench'.

"Come and sit down" Maria said still holding Philip's large hands tightly in her own small ones; she was not going to let him go, her precious boy deserved more than this. An idea formed in her mind, as she smiled and took in the changes of his face.

"My baby boy" she said.

"Mama I'm not such a baby anymore." Philip said laughing, he felt safer when she was there, and he reverted back to being a young child as his mother's love washed over him like a balm. It cured everything, it always did.

"You will always be my baby," Maria stated.

The sun slowly made its way across the sky from

east to west. Neither noticed its progress as they told each other of their day-to-day lives. Occasionally one would get a drink from the dispensary, but not one moment was wasted as they sat and talked.

Philip was always interested in his mother's life; it seemed so exciting and entertaining. Nowadays she specialised in trying to collate information from old food sources such as potatoes, not many varieties had survived. Many of the plants were now cloned to bring back food sources that were safe to eat. Philip always thought how ironic it was, what his mother did for a living.

He had asked her why she was inseminated with him; he had heard what many of his friend's mothers had done. Some were horrific and a lot of their boys didn't want anything to do with their mothers. After all, they were still their Mothers'. He had built himself up over the months to have the courage to ask his mother, he didn't want it to be bad. He hoped she was a victim of the pyramid as many were. His relief when she explained was palpable, but the injustice of it all he felt more deeply than most.

"You seem lost in thought," Maria stated. "Just thinking about how hard it must be in hiding me out there". He said, pointing towards the perimeter.

"You would be surprised, not all women have children, most I meet presume I have none so I don't say, and I wish I could tell people how beautiful baby boy has grown into a wonderful son. I'm so proud of you; please don't ever think I'm not". She looked at him.

"I don't ever regret having you" she paused "you are the reason I live day to day, you bring me happiness every moment of my life." She laughed and it reached her eyes "I don't have to share you with anyone".

"But Mama, without me you would have a

prestigious career and be out of that apartment you keep in the city". He said regretting his mother's misfortunes and thinking of his own.

"This may be, but I would not have the love I have felt with you and special moments". She smiled. "In fact before I came in the garden I was remembering the time we picked the grapes and watched clouds. I would not have those special moments in my life and I would be worse off for it". She looked at him; I still wish to change the world to make it better for you, that hope has never left me". "I have nothing to say to that". He plainly stated. "I have vague memories of when I was small, mainly of sitting on your knee and the feeling of not being scared or alone". "You are never alone, I am always there". She gently touched his chest where his heart was beating". I told you this when they took you away from me. Philip smiled.

"I love you Mama" he stated simply. "I love you too darling". Maria gave him a gentle hug. He seemed low today – she knew why, but she didn't wish for him to remember the bad times when he was with her.

"Hey do you still look at the moon, like I said to you when you were a little boy? Maria asked. "Of course I do – it doesn't matter where you are or where I am we can both see the moon". He laughed. "Good, because I still look at the moon every night and wish you a good night". He laughed. "So do I, but don't tell the men in here as it sounds so childish.

"Who cares what people think" Maria said, "the moon is there every night and I wish I could have been there for you too". She looked at her son "Come here and give your mother a cuddle, I miss you everyday". After the intenseness of the moment, Maria thought he needed to walk away from this place. "Come let's go for a walk before dinner is served and I have to go".

"Don't mention the day is drifting by, let's enjoy the

110

moment". He stood up "that walk sounds a good idea it's getting crowded in the garden." They both walked down the path towards the shelter of the woodland. Maria still held his hand as if he were a small child.

They walked around the woods the sun dappling on the ground in front of them. The shade was a relief from the sun. Neither wished to go inside, they used to but it became harder for them both to see where Philip was living. It was so institutionalised in an unsaid agreement between themselves they stayed outside and there time together was not imposed on by anyone else. It was their time and it was special to them. The time ticked by quicker than they both wished, sometimes they walked in a comfortable silence just wondering around enjoying each other's company. It felt like a dark cloud hanging over them knowing there time together would end and soon, until the next visit.

"Do you need anything bringing next time?" Maria asked. She used to bring him sweets, goodies and toys now she struggled.

"I am running out of soaps and toiletries" he said thinking of the small teddy in his room he had kept since he was a small boy, a reminder of his Mama. "I will look for something special". Maria said, "you need things now you have grown up". She laughed hollowly "even though I try not to admit it". The bell rang echoing fear, hitting Maria in the stomach, she didn't want to leave him this time more than ever. He was her precious boy and she had no control over what happened to him. She felt sick. Seeing the look on his mother's face, he recognised her agony.

"I will be fine" he said "I will be more careful in the gym" he said smiling making light of his injuries wondering if he could avoid anymore of the party scene.

"I know you will" Maria said giving her son a huge

hug, Philip winced. "Oh I am sorry didn't mean to hug you so tightly".

"It wouldn't be the same if you didn't," he said as he rubbed his side. The bell rang again.

"Come, I will walk with you to the doors" Philip said. They walked as slow as possible to where the guards stood waiting to rip them apart again.

"It will be okay you know". Maria stated. Philip had never seen such determination on her face. He wondered what she meant it was not like her. "I know Mama" he said, "you must go" he pointed over to the guards "they will complain". Giving him one last hug, she looked up to his face. "I love you darling," she said. "I love you too Mama" he said regrettably Maria turned away she waved as she walked back into the grey room. Philip stood waiting until he could see her no more as he always had since being small.

Maria waved again and he returned the wave both mouthing I love you as she turned to walk away from the enclosure. Philip meandered towards his room even at eighteen he needed to cry each time she left.

"Get me Erin Holt" Maria said into her personal wrist computer as she left the compound.

"Maria" Erin appeared before her "how can I help?"

"Philip needs to get out of there. This cannot happen to him again". Anger emanated from her palpably.

"You okay?" Erin asked her confused.

"I will be with your help". Maria stated. "Meet me later we need to talk" Maria ended the communication abruptly. Erin would understand this had to stop it just had to – he was her precious boy she forgot about saving the world she now had to save her son.

14

Natasha looked up at the vast white building looming above her she hated this, no one knew about her mother especially as she had changed her surname to Simpson. She loved the medic at the children's home where she grew up. It was the only remnant of her past she acknowledged. Once she became eighteen and came into her trust fund, those doors on her past were closed forever and with it went her name. The indescribable feeling of being ripped away from her mother made her feel, nothing could hurt her anymore. Hardening herself, she walked into the stark clinical institution.

A lady sat behind a desk in an empty corridor, although Natasha was the only other person in the room she didn't look up from what she was reading.

"Excuse me?" Natasha stated to get her attention.

"One moment" the lady held up her hand for Natasha to be quiet. Irritation rippled through Natasha but she knew from experience it was no use arguing. She waited pacing up and down in front of the doors, for what seemed to be an age, there were no chairs to sit on. The lady looked up at her walking on the marble floor not once did Natasha look in her direction.

"Can I help you?" she asked Natasha in a brusque manner. On hearing her Natasha who had no thoughts running through her head, was just trying to harden herself to what was to come.

"Yes please" Natasha said sarcasm dripping from her every pore. "I have come to see Vanessa Gresval."

"Name?" The officious woman asked.

"Natasha Simpson" she replied.

"Relationship?" the woman asked her.

"Daughter" Natasha hated having to explain herself to this over eager person in front of her. The lady raised

113

an eyebrow at Natasha. She had been here before always due to her name change, it was not for her to judge.

"Natasha Simpson, is here to visit, Vanessa Gresval can I send her through?" The woman seemed to be talking to herself from where Natasha was standing she knew the comms system was so old there were no holographic communications.

"Send her through now." The voice echoed in the empty hall.

"You can go through to the visitor's room now."

"I heard" Natasha was sharp.

"Do you know where you are going?"

"Unfortunately, yes I do." Natasha replied.

"Please go through" Natasha walked past into the empty hall it echoed like a cathedral. Walking to the end there were double doors. She stood not going through them, breathing deeply and slowly she waited it was as if she was covering herself in a force field to protect herself. Steeling herself visibly she pushed open the doors.

Inside it was if she had walked into a wall, the noise was deafening. The medics were trying to contain the patients, some screamed, some were talking gibberish others just sat staring. Scanning the room, she was looking for a dark haired woman. This place sent a shiver of fear through her although many were animated, what scared her was there was nothing in their eyes. The drugs being fed to them on an hourly basis seemed to take their soles each time one was administered. In the corner, she found who she was looking for, evading contact with the other patients, she weaved her way to her mother. As usual, she sat quietly in the corner; her eyes were glazed along with the others. Next to her was a medic she sat quietly holding her hand.

"How had she been?" no need for introductions or formalities.

"She has been asking for you," Lily stated.

"I wish I could visit more often Lily – you know what work is like" Natasha didn't expand; they both knew it was a lie. Lily had been looking after Vanessa since she had come to the institution eighteen years ago. She watched the young woman before her, grow from an innocent spoilt young girl to the hard woman she saw before her. Examining Natasha as she stood there occasionally there were glimpses of that young girl.

"Mother?" Natasha squatted down before Vanessa. She was a shell of the woman she once was. Her hair although clean was lank and had no life in it; it fell in a curtain down her back. Her once healthy glow was long gone into a drawn pallor. Her back was hunched where she had given up any semblance of fight she once had.

"Mother?" A drawn smile appeared on Vanessa's face.

"My baby" she said a glimmer of recognition appeared in her eyes. Natasha didn't know what to say she couldn't ask how she was.

"Yes Mummy – I am here" Natasha smiled but it didn't reach her eyes.

"My beautiful girl" Vanessa said.

"She should be quite chatty her medication is wearing off in this last hour she always becomes more talkative." Lily butting in the tender moment between mother and daughter. "She does tend to talk about all sorts of thing, don't let it upset you." Natasha nodded.

"I miss you," Natasha whispered.

"Don't let them get you too," Vanessa said in conspirital tones.

"No one has got me Mummy" Natasha was used to her digressing.

"Be careful tell no one about the anomaly" Vanessa started to shake.

"Mummy you know there is no anomaly"

"But there is" Vanessa said, "That's why I am here." Sadness entered her eyes Natasha could hardly bear it.

"My beautiful girl – be safe – pyramid dangerous"

"Mummy – you know I work there I have just had a promotion my boss is Erin Holt". Natasha said smiling.

"No must get away," Vanessa said, "protect you"

"Is she babbling again?" Lily asked.

"Unfortunately yes – thought she was with us for a moment," Natasha said talking over Vanessa's head to Lily, still holding her mother's hands.

Vanessa looked at her daughter she was so proud of her. Her head was fuzzy, she couldn't think straight there was so much to tell her but she couldn't remember.

"Mummy it is ok – I love you," she whispered so Lily couldn't hear her.

"I love you too darling," Vanessa said for a moment she was herself clear "be safe tell no one."

"I won't, I promise Mummy" tears pricked at Natasha's eyes. Steadily Natasha stood and bent over giving her mother a cuddle, she smelt of disinfectant not the perfume she remembered as a child. She remembered that safe feeling as the smell wafted over her embraced in her mother's arms. That was long gone now. Tears flowed silently down Natasha cheeks; pulling herself together, the tears still glistened in her eyes and on the back of her hands where she had wiped them away hastily.

"I almost forgot" she rummaged in her bag trying to find a small box "here I bought this I found some in the apothecary's the other day." Natasha pulled out a small gold box opening it she pulled out a bottle with amber liquid inside. Carefully Natasha pulled off the lid.

"Mummy pass me your hand" Natasha pulled Vanessa's arm towards her spraying the perfume on her wrist, them she repeated the action with her other wrist.

"Smell it mummy it's the perfume you always wore – I found some for you" Natasha manoeuvred her mother's arm so she could smell her wrist. Apprehensively Vanessa smelled the aroma – new to her but so familiar she smiled at the daughter and a single tear ran down her cheek.

"Are you OK?" Natasha was horrified Vanessa nodded happiness flooded through her eyes them they filled with regret.

"You like it?" Natasha asked, then Vanessa did something rare she touched her daughters face with tenderness her eyes full of recognition the drugs were wearing off she could think clearly.

"My beautiful girl" Vanessa said, "thank you" was all she could say her mouth would not co-operate with what she had started to think. Natasha smiled sincerely for the first time in so long it felt unnatural.

"It is a pleasure I would do anything for you Mummy" she paused hoping she was still with her, "I love you so much".

"I love you too," Vanessa said then very quietly and making sure Lily was out of earshot. "Help me".

The medication trolley was being wheeled around the room slowly as each patient took their individual doses the room became quieter.

"What do you mean?"

"Get me out – the anomaly we are it."

"Mummy I don't know what you mean?" Natasha stated confused – it wasn't like normal, she seemed sane although each movement was still slow.

"Your medicines are here, Vanessa," Lily stated. "All this excitement you could do with a nap"

"Wait" Natasha said holding her hand up to Lily as

she was trying to pass Vanessa her medication. Making sure she had her mother's full attention "Mummy I will try my best."

Vanessa nodded and obediently took the pills – slowly the glazed look in her eyes returned. Natasha felt sick she normally dealt with it better than this, it was easier when she didn't seem so lucid.

The bottle of perfume was still in her hand, she passed it to Lily for safekeeping.

"Spray this on her every day, I don't wish for her to smell like this institution anymore." Natasha looked pointedly at the bottle, "I will bring some more next time I come," she informed Lily. Turning to Vanessa Natasha bent down to her ear. "Mummy I am going now" Natasha said, having no response as Vanessa's eyes started to close. Giving her a brief cuddle, she straightened herself and nodded to Lily as a goodbye. Her eyes filled, and she couldn't say anything if she wanted to.

Steadying herself she walked through the double doors and walked down the marble hall tears flowed as her quick footsteps echoed in the hall. She seemed as if she had tunnel vision heading to the glass entrance pushing her way through them she took a deep breath of air as she soaked up the sun.

15

Erin walked to work from where she lived she found it more convenient, better than getting the hover. Her offices stood on the Straights of Birmingham (apparently named after some ancient city that was there before the great floods). It was beautiful looking over woodland not close enough inside the mainland to be claustrophobic – a pretty building with glass windows mirrored of course – one would not want to see inside. She smiled everyday passing the hover launch pads and the aeronautical pads. She felt supercilious as she entered the building. She had never mixed home life with work – she had good reason. Maria turning up yesterday concerned her, it could jeopardise her career.

Overall, it was innocent; she had not been to dinner for ages. Could be Phillip nearly twenty appalled her it made her feel old.

Entering her office the blue wall flickered into life.

"You are late!" Was written on the wall at the same time a simulated voice reiterated what it said.

"It doesn't matter, I am the boss." Erin snapped. "Do you have to write everything you say – it's beneath you – you know?"

"I manage well" computer replied.

"Desist with the niceties – anything to report?" Erin hated mornings.

"Not of importance – security code please?"

"Ok you can tell me that I am late but I still have to give you my clearance – It is getting monotonous you know."

"Security clearance please."

"7211396" Erin spat.

"Thank you – only following procedures."

"For a computer you can be really sarcastic." She flicked through her messages. "Computer have there been any incidents lately?"

"One ma'am. Two guards have been removed from the Lakes." The computer replied.

"What for?" Erin knew they had bad problems with guards in the past – some were overzealous.

"Raping one of the men and various other activities."

"Such as?"

"Making the men have intercourse with each other, while the guards watched."

"Only two? Are they the ring leaders?" Erin hated cases like these; it made her feel guilty about Phillip. Although she had got him into the enclosure with a decent reputation – of course close enough for Maria to visit.

"Yes" the computer replied.

"Report please" on the wall Erin saw the women who had committed the crime – for a punishment they were sent for hard labour. "Please type a memo to all heads of prisons – Anyone caught abusing the specimens will be extremely punished. Have Faith examine it." There was a knock at the door. The wall immediately became blank. Natasha walked into the room.

"Hello madam, I realise I am new in the department so I thought I would hold a dinner party. I would be most grateful if you would come." Natasha didn't like her new boss and wanted promotion out of home affairs – quickly. Everyone was far too straight.

"I'm sorry Natasha, it was a lovely offer but I don't mix work with my social life – anyway I find everyone has more fun when I'm not there." Erin had heard of Natasha's parties. They were not her thing she would have to work hard, as did everyone in her department to gain promotion not to gain favours.

"I don't want to be presumptuous – but don't underestimate yourself madam. Everyone really likes you." Natasha was getting desperate six months in the department not once had she been to any of her parties. "If you don't wish to come alone bring a friend – yes that one who came yesterday – sorry I didn't catch, what is it you said she did?" Erin caught on the defensive.

"Micro biologist" She replied.

"What a wonderful position – yes do bring her. She would be a very interesting guest." Natasha smiled serenely. "Anyway the party is tomorrow 19.30 hours. I'll see you there." Erin watched as Natasha waltzed out of her office; sure, she had never accepted, Maria was going to freak. All those people –she was near enough a hermit these days. Ceres would have to persuade her to come – Erin knew Natasha enough to know she was dangerous.

"Computer, contact Ceres Zanuti in the Main frame department."

"How do I look, I hate things like this why does Natasha want me to go anyway?" Maria smoothed down her silver dress it had a cast of blue when she walked.

"Firstly you look fine – anyone would with your figure – sickly." Erin laughed at her own joke. Maria just frowned.

"Anyway I'm not sure why, Natasha thinks she knows something. I am not sure it is Phillip but it may be about your past, I don't like her in my department. She's conniving – I've asked Ceres to check my computer she's got it encoded, I don't like this at all." Erin mused.

"You seem very determined about this don't you –
you are getting repetitive in your old age – you've told
me you don't like her twice." Maria commented, seeing
faint lines forming around her eyes as she glanced
again, unsure, in the mirror.

"I'm nervous and jumpy," Erin snapped.

"What if someone, gets hold of our past. I'd be
ruined, all that work we did" Maria came over and gave
Erin a hug.

As usual, Erin was thinking of herself Maria was not
keen on hearing Natasha's latest exploit, Erin had pre-
warned her of what the night may consist of. She was
not impressed, all these years of trying to move on,
although her life revolved around her son and those
precious visits. Maria mused walking out of the
apartment, following Erin to her hover. Nothing much
had changed Maria liked the comfort of her old things
that surrounded her; there was still a box of toys piled
underneath the many books (she was old fashioned that
way). A small reminder that a little boy once ran
around her now shabby home. She lived for her visits to
see how he has grown, her heart ripped out of her each
time she left.

Before she knew it they arrived at the apartment, her
palms were sweaty at the thought.

*Pull yourself together woman for goodness sake you
are nearly forty*, she thought despondently. Wondering
what it would be like this evening, it didn't seem to be
her idea of a night out.

"Hello" the door answered their knock, a face appeared
two feet from where they stood.

"Party guests?" The face questioned them, Erin
nudged Maria.

"Natasha is doing well that's the latest model." Erin
muttered under her breath.

"Do you wish for me to impart this information to Natasha?" The hovering head asked, it had a quizzical look on its holographic face.

"Oh no thank you," Erin replied laughing, she composed herself "a party guest, yes? Maria Stevenson and Erin Holt."

"Please pass, Natasha's expecting you" the head evaporated into the ether and the door slid automatically into its housing above, leaving Erin and Maria to see freely into her house. They obviously were not the first to arrive; various women were talking to each other in clear view of the door. Erin noticed they were all high up in the pyramid.

"It may not be a useless evening after all," Erin whispered to Maria.

"You will never change." Maria whispered back.

"Natasha is not the only one with ambition". Erin said raising one eyebrow smiling widely.

Natasha definitely wished to impress, Natasha looked striking in her gold spray leaving little to the imagination, as she was naked. The house had informed her of their arrival she made her way over to them, smiling as she walked, Erin's smile was fixed painfully, and her dislike was growing rapidly.

"Erin – darling thank you so much for endearing us with your presence, this must be Maria" she paused only for a second not giving Erin time to reply. "So glad to meet you at last. Heard so much about you - please have drinks" she turned to find two glasses of champagne appear from a compartment in the wall. Both women looked apprehensively at the contents of their glasses now firmly in their grasp.

"You must drink, got a slight kick if you know what I mean" Winking at them, Natasha turned and left with a flourish to entertain her other guests.

Erin turned to Maria in conspirital tones.

"Not quite the way one would treat ones boss!" Imitating Natasha's supercilious tone, Maria sniggered into her glass. "Self confident isn't she" slightly raising her eyebrow.

Natasha's penetrating voice again interrupted them as it was amplified to get everyone's attention.

"Everyone please eat, the entertainment will soon be displayed." Natasha laughed; as did all the other guests, they parted slightly to let the table rise from the floor fully laden with food.

"Should we grab some food?" Maria suggested, "better fit in, they all seem to be old acquaintances."

They walked over to the rest of the company trying to avoid bumping into anyone. "The food looks good I am impressed. Erin picked up a small fish, taking a tentative bite. "Nice" she handed one to Maria.

"Come on a better talk to these people" Erin said.

"If I must" Maria smiled" following Erin's lead, they gently ingratiated themselves to the other guests. They kept the topics to work – which was extremely easy as most were Erin's work colleagues. The Pyramid kept their relations with the masses to a minimum. Most were surprised at Erin's appearance but they were soon accepted, realising Natasha was now in her department.

"You are in for a lovely treat, Natasha always seems to pick well" a lady glided up behind them. Erin knew her she was called Sabrina. She was obviously enjoying Natasha's 'pick me up' drinks. They were not common anymore since the climate change, most drank water. Erin was surprised at the lady's appearance at the party as much as Sabrina was of her. She was a well respected agricultural minister.

Erin nudged Maria warning her of the advancing

Natasha. "Sabrina, I'm so pleased you've found Erin and Maria" she smiled at them all. "Excuse me a moment I just need to announce the entertainment."

Again, Natasha's voice rang over the crowd.

"Find a comfortable position, the entertainment is about to begin. Erin nudged Maria "stay for a while and then we'll slip out – work commitments or something." Maria rolled her eyes, the lighting dimmed everyone grabbed a large cushion from the pile they hadn't noticed in the corner, the other guests sat down.

Natasha guided them. "Please make yourself comfortable; I'm sure you will love my entertainment – if I say so myself, it is quite renowned." Natasha left them holding their cushions, to usher the other guests to the cushions.

Erin was paying special interest in her activities; she was talking to her in house computer. Play latest acquirement to my collection. A light shone on Natasha and again her voice amplified. "Ladies – enjoy" she then disappeared into the surrounding darkness.

"She likes that doesn't she," Maria laughed into Erin's ear. Horror seemed to slide onto her face like a mask. Her attitude soon changed as she looked at the wall in front of her.

"For God's sake, smile and don't move" Erin spat at Maria through smiling teeth. Maria just stared and followed Erin's instructions as a girl would a mother – on automatic. The show was Phillip from that mornings encounter.

Natasha watched them from a safe distance not to be seen; they knew him, why and how? Another visit was necessary, private, no cameras, maybe just once. She had to make an exception, she would get out of that department and soon, she had tried being nice. Anyway, it would not be such an unpleasant experience, she thought. If they think this is not to their liking they certainly will not approve of the second part of the evening. Natasha smiled to herself disappearing to enjoy her private evening's entertainment before the visual finished.

Phillip was stripping off his clothes, the camera zooming in on his muscles gently moving down to his groin – the party atmosphere seemed to be catching giggles emanating around the room. Erin undid her outfit with an expertise any stripper would be proud of; she performed well smiling confidentially to the camera, stroking Phillip making sure he was in full camera shot. Phillip was definitely the centre of attention. A zoo exhibit. He looked robotic no expression reaching his climax after performing his duty. Natasha seemed pleased with the reaction as she re-entered the room. Her voice that was pre-recorded, unknown to the guests, was overheard as a commentary to the scenes on the visual.

"Don't you think he has a large penis?"

"Isn't he clever" when he performed to their liking.

"Has been taught well – must give his tutor a promotion" the audience laughed at all the smoothly rehearsed places. The rest approved and clapped when Phillip gave Natasha an oral climax. Maria felt sick, Erin held her in place, bruising her arm. As it ended Natasha's voice again was heard, Erin was sighing with relief she had managed to keep Maria relatively calm.

"I thought another visit was appropriate, this was a little tame, break him in." The other guests clapped and nodded their approval. "Now ladies we have a speciality for you this evening, you all must thank my boss" Erin was none too amused but as she was surrounded by the very people who could ruin her; she played along with Natasha's charade, smiling to the other guests. Now she was concerned.

126

"Please let me introduce a light entertainment for you this evening" A line of people entered the room all of male gender all from the enclosure. Erin was furious now she knew why Natasha was eager to get into her department it was slightly more than a career move. Maria's eyes were like saucers looking for Phillip. Erin was praying he was not there. He was not - both exhaled with relief both terrified of the same thing. Erin suddenly came back to focus, many of the women had disappeared some together and some with a male.

"Time to leave" she dragged Maria to her feet, "Smile!"

"Natasha" Erin called over to Natasha, on hearing her name she came over to them,

"Must go early start." As an afterthought, she added, "the entertainment was very revealing," she laughed.

"I am so pleased you enjoyed it," Natasha purred, "I thought a rather good specimen" She smiled not letting them answer. "He was particularly well built; I'll give you his enclosure and number at work tomorrow. I do recommend a visit." Natasha paused.

"I think we must go, I have an early appointment in the morning" Erin smiled.

"Don't you want to stay here? Most of my guests do, you know." Natasha laughed at something that looked like it had just crossed her mind "I have toys you know, you and your friend can play with, if you would prefer to be alone, I think the men have all been monopolised." She smiled at them.

"That would be a very tempting offer on another day perhaps but work as always must come first" Erin sighed for effect, "highly disappointing sometimes I must say." Erin declined as best she could. If she was going to pull this off, she needed to get Maria out and fast.

"Are you sure? I've a small private gathering in my

own room." Natasha was nearly insistent – but not quite. "I am sorry I didn't OK the males with you but I thought you wouldn't mind – we all take some liberties with the job, don't we?" Natasha left the comment hanging in the air – Erin didn't like her tone.

"Natasha – Darling" Sabrina was calling from the other part of the room.

"I see you're wanted, don't worry we will see ourselves out." Erin's arm was under Maria's waist literally holding her up. The door opened as they went outside the hologram appeared. Natasha wishes to invite you to the next party. She wishes it to be called The Next Instalment."

"That would be lovely" Erin replied.

"I will tell her" the face dissipated, Maria collapsed into her arms, they were not safe yet.

"Maria!" Erin smacked her face hard – no one must see. Pulling her up, they got into the hover. Erin's mind was in overdrive; she *is more dangerous than I thought* – Maria's mind had shut down not being able to cope with what she saw.

"I will visit him" Erin's comments went unheard as they headed for home.

Natasha entered her bedroom Phillip lay naked on her bed – bored. Her "toys" were scattered around the room.

"Phillip – darling I've got a few friends they'll be here in a minute – you must entertain them or life will become extremely difficult for you. Do we understand each other?"

Phillip nodded his head slightly, to show her he understood what was expected of him.

16

Erin had never really looked inside the enclosures before. From the outside it was surrounded by scrubland. The entrance buried into the rock an electrical field surrounded the grounds where the men were allowed to walk, unseen from the naked eye. Erin contacted the guards inside.

"Mendip – security clearance" Erin spoke into her communicator, there was no reply. The red light on her wrist changed to green indicating she could pass through the invisible barrier. As she got closer to the entrance the protective shield shimmered maneuvering her hover towards what seemed to be just another beautiful view, but she knew the 'insignificant door' would soon be in sight. The glass panels seemed to be set into the countryside. Leaving the hover at the docking bay, she walked over to the doors. The heat was making Erin perspire. The doors parted into their encasements hidden in the rock as she approached. A guard came out to greet her.

"Ma'am – it is a pleasure for you to honour us in this way." Quite obviously, the guard had confirmed her identity and hoped it was not a security breach. Erin used her security band to identify the guard it scanned her facial features.

"Jacqueline – that will be fine – I've come on a recommendation of an employee" Erin watched the guards face change from fear to a knowing smile – Erin preferred the fear.

"Come this way Ma'am?" Jacqueline asked, "Is there anyone in particular you would like to see?"

"Actually yes – X1250246" Erin replied.

"His popularity has recently raised Ma'am, Would you like to see another Ma'am – They're all the same."

"No" Erin snapped "He will do – just fetch him." Erin was getting irritated "Now!" The guard ushered Erin into an empty room – she just waited as the guard scuttled off to collect Phillip.

Time seemed to stop as she waited, what was she to say? He would not remember her – does she say anything or just see if he is all right.

"Ma'am" Erin was disturbed from her reverie, as Jacqueline had returned.

"Yes" Erin replied occasionally she enjoyed the benefits of being the boss.

"Would you follow me please, the specimen is waiting," Erin followed her through the white sterilised corridor into another room identical to the last, but this one had a circular bed in the centre and Phillip was standing in the far corner.

"Any requests Ma'am before you enter, Erin was interested in what seemed common place to the guard.

"We could record the action for you and deliver it to your Personal computer." Jacqueline paused "We have a variety of implements Ma'am"

"Such as?" Erin was starting to feel uneasy about this.

"Knives, handcuffs, tape, Vaseline, various foodstuffs."

"Stop – None of the above – thank you" Erin was amazed by the amount and the way in which she recalled them – she was repelled at the way these men were treated.

"I do request one thing I don't wish to be recorded – even for security" Erin considered the guard "my reputation you understand."

"Yes Ma'am" the guard left and the door slid into place. Erin used her security to close the door – total privacy.

Phillip saw this and contemplated this woman, she

looked vaguely familiar, and he hoped not one of Natasha's colleagues. He stood awaiting his instructions recent experiences had made him weary.

"Please sit" Erin commanded as she looked around the room feeling extremely uncomfortable.

"Do you want me to take off my clothes?" Phillip questioned, disconcerted, most of them who visited him knew what they wanted, this one was difficult – something about her looked familiar, Erin checked her Personal computer on her wrist."

"Computer – check the room is secure"

"Camera recording" it answered.

"Shut them down secure doors" Erin ordered.

"Complete"

"Shut down" the computer screen flashed instantaneously – the small screen blacked out. Phillip was weary, this one was obsessed with privacy, God what was she going to do with him he wondered, backing off slightly into the corner. Erin visibly relaxed.

"Please sit down Phillip."

"How do you know my name? You are not one of Natasha's cronies are you?" He didn't like this, his body was still sore from the party. He secretly hoped Natasha and her friends had already bored of him.

"Actually Natasha works for me" Erin smiled but she was horrified as an involuntary groan emitted from Phillip.

"Don't worry I am friends with your mother." She paused Phillip was still not relaxing, not sitting down.

"Please relax, I'm not here for 'pleasures' her distaste was visible on her face. "I am here just to check how you are" Phillip relaxed slightly and sat down still suspicion ran through his eyes. He wanted to know how his mother was and was intrigued why Erin was here. As he sat, he winced from the pain – his ribs were broken and the lacerations were not healing as quickly as he would like.

"Are you alright?" Erin asked, seeing the pain fleeting across his face.

"Yes I'm fine"

"Take that top off."Phillip stood back up, he was worried.

"It isn't like that" Erin dismayed "I've known you since you were brought home by your mother – eurgh." Walking over to him with some force, she pushed him back into the chair. Then unexpectedly ruffled his hair.

A distant memory came to Phillip he remembered two women always at his Mum's home the only home he had ever felt safe. With help from Erin, he removed his shirt.

"My God" Erin exclaimed, "who did this to you?"

"Your colleague and her friends" Phillip said bitterness creeping into his voice. "Apparently she knows you; she said you had given permission for the activities." Phillip said showing his distaste to Erin. How could his mother associate with people like her, Erin didn't know what to say.

Erin was was horrified but she didn't want Phillip to know that both Maria and herself were at that party, he would feel let down. Erin wondered where he was at the part, she never saw him.

"Have you had these treated?" She asked Phillip to hide her confusion.

"Yes but they are not healing too well" He paused examining a particularly bad laceration on his stomach, the stitches were pulling apart "they said they are growing some skin to hide this he said, pointing to the stitches." Phillip and Erin looked around the room not sure of what to do or say next.

"I'm going to be checked over when we leave here, wouldn't it be a good idea if we actually did have intercourse" Phillip asked matter-of-factly.

"I couldn't" Erin exclaimed horrified at the thought. "You are Maria's son"

"So, it made no difference to anyone else" he shrugged "what's the problem? In the last century before all this, he spread his arms around. They used to have intercourse and pleasure themselves all the time." He smiled "we did it in sex lessons. His attitude disarmed Erin he looked so vulnerable. Although she was not in the least bit attracted to him, he did remind her of Maria.

"It would be a better cover," she said "But I'm sorry I can't do that, it is so wrong" Erin stated, recovering quickly from the embarrassment she continued.

"I need to tell you this, don't tell Maria I came, she's not coping too well at the moment."

"That's – no problem she is only allowed to visit rarely. Apparently it's bad for my welfare if she comes too often." The sarcasm had a bitter edge to it coming from Phillip.

Erin looked into his face, older than his years etched into his features. She had to sort this mess; it was her and Ceres that had bullied Maria into this, now look at it! Phillip was confused.

"What will I say?"

"Just say I was strange and wished to look at you naked." Erin replied.

"After the experiences I have had lately that would be a pleasure". A grin lit up his face.

"It will get better, I promise you it will."

As Erin left the confinement of the room, Jacqueline was waiting outside.

"Jacqueline" Erin uttered.

"Yes ma'am."

"Make sure no more visitations are made to him, I want him for my own personal amusement."

"Consider it done." That can easily be arranged a promotion might be appropriated to her if she did as she asked. Pleased with herself she let Erin into the entrance hall.

Natasha had a day off she wanted to enjoy it – Phillip was getting better trained but she was not used to being kept waiting. The guard had been evasive; making her wait in this room, if she was not careful she would be demoted. It could soon be arranged. Getting irritated Natasha paced around the room. The door opened and Erin who was mortified about the whole experience walked straight into Natasha.

"Oh – are you waiting for me?" Erin asked knowing the answer.

"No ma'am – it's my day off" Natasha replied

"I find Phillip fascinating, sorry to spoil your entertainment but I've ordered him to be kept from other visitations – I like keeping him to myself." Erin smiled.

"I'll have to find another toy," Natasha said obviously rattled. "I was getting bored of him anyway – Good luck ma'am – I hope I trained him well." A smirk crossed her face

"Yes – I think you did a very good job on his training" Erin paused "I'd better get off" as an afterthought, she barely remembered the previous evening. "I heard Michael is very good." Erin didn't acknowledge but walked off leaving Natasha standing there. She left, she needed to speak to Ceres, this had to stop.

Ceres walked to work. It wasn't far, the mainframe stood in the centre of the city. She hated her job, she was not as clever as Maria nor as ambitious as Erin, yes she knew her job but it wasn't pleasant. She pondered

134

how three highly idealistic individuals had come to this. *What had happened?* She and Erin were the lucky ones – they had missed the lottery. She had her suspicions about that, Erin meddled when it suited her. Although having a girl was not her idea of fun. Since the accident, all genealogy had been banned, later other excuses were used, lack of budget or something of that nature. Typical, just as they had started to replicate the womb. She had seen others pregnant not only Maria. Bodies distorted, at least the others had gone to the convalescing institute, she had heard of women who had been punished but they were rare.

Walking through the entrance Ceres was always amazed how innocent it looked all she could see was a beautiful garden filled with specimen trees (ones that had almost been wiped out by the flood: oranges, limes and cherry trees). In the centre was a copy of a roman temple. The marble steps lead into a square, Ceres headed towards the left, to the right was the pyramid Ceres took her normal action of ignoring everyone as she passed into the hub of the nation – the mainframe.

Ceres sat at her desk – she was supposed to be reprogramming a new system for the justice praeposters.

"Message from Praeposter's S16" her computer reminded her.

"Hi Ceres – I have an idea." Erin appeared in front of her. "I'll meet you there in an hour" Erin's holographic image disappeared just as quickly as it had appeared. Ceres sighed after what had happened to Maria, Erin sounded as if she had another scheme – she couldn't be that idiotic. Ceres supposed she had better finish her program, she was not normally this enthusiastic but she didn't know what Erin was up to.

The hour passed without incident.

"Ceres" Erin whispered.

"God, don't do that" Ceres was startled, Erin appeared in person straight in front of her desk.

"How did you get in here? I did the security myself?" Ceres muttered and quietly she was hurt it failed.

"Excellent job if I say so" Erin smiled "for God's sake do you forget who I work for? I've top security clearance"

"I wasn't thinking" Ceres said slightly relieved.

"Is this a social visit? I could with some lunch"

"Yes, get your things; I will pass on your excuses to your boss" Erin winked "Oh I forgot I already have." Erin smiled "Come on before they suspect anything." Ceres noticed Erin was carrying a yellow bag.

"You are slipping" Ceres said pointing to the bag "doesn't quite match the outfit."

"Lunch" Erin replied. They walked through the office no one took any notice most were engrossed with their work trying to gain promotion, very few people were actually in the office as most worked from home when they chose. Ceres preferred the company it gave her an incentive to actually do something.

Outside they sat at the edge of the garden. "Communicator block signals to impulses code X3"

"Complete"

"Shut down" Erin said to her personal computer on her wrist. "Right down to business – it's Phillip" Erin handed Ceres a piece of food from her bag.

"What's this?" Ceres curled her lip.

"It's a sandwich, my mother used to make them, just take a bite."

"Not bad, strange but not bad, what has happened with Phillip?" Ceres said, "Maria would not answer her communicator yesterday"

"Well, Natasha held a party as you know, she wished to meet Maria, that is what I'm worried about."

Erin wondered aloud.

"Why?"

"I'm not sure – call it a gut feeling- I've been in this job too long now not to worry, I think Phillip is being used as one of Natasha's pets."

"A what?" Ceres was starting to get a sickly feeling in her stomach.

"You couldn't get hold of Maria yesterday?" Erin's mind wandered back to the previous conversation.

"Stop digressing" Ceres said, "What's this about pets?"

"Well, it's common knowledge about the pyramid and their sexual appetites – they class it as a bonus. Anyway, Natasha has been promoted within the pyramid quickly and she has ended up in my department. Trying to impress me I think, either that or she's after my job which is more likely. I've got a feeling she knows something about Phillip, what it is I am not sure but she was adamant I brought Maria."

"Has she found out about Maria's past?"

"I'm not sure – but I think Maria gave herself away when we watched Phillip at the party – I get the feeling Natasha was watching her."

"I'll do some digging in the system I might find a glitch in the program. She might find out that way." Ceres thought aloud "Just let us hope to God someone from our past has not resurfaced."

"Can I leave this with you I'm going to check out her past – It'll be a routine check – I like to know where people in my department have come from – that lady needs her security clearance – it will be a good cover."

17

"X1250246, to entrance" Phillip was on his bed mulling over what his mother's friend told him. His scars were healing slowly, Natasha was a vicious cow.

"X1250246 to Entrance!" the voice reverberated around his room – they must be desperate, he thought to himself. He pulled himself off his bed and stood by his entrance to his room. The mirrored door way shimmered and slid upwards revealing two guards in front of it.

"Hi Phillip," the smaller of the two spoke first, he recognized Jenny she supervised his corridor, Phillip smiled.

"What's it this time, extracurricular perks?" he was used to these late night calls as he was a particular favourite of Jenny's. Her friend – he'd not seen before, must want to join in. His thoughts were cut short.

"Confirm number." The other guard commanded ignoring his joke – Jenny did look a bit harassed.

"X1250246" Phillip replied, he hoped she was not the type that was into strange sexual exploits – he had enough of them recently. Jenny's face was starting to get flustered – not something official.

"Please pack your belongings," Jenny asked. As an afterthought to impress the other guard, "you have 5 minutes"

"I can't. Where am I going?" Phillip was getting annoyed.

"Removal to another enclosure" the officious guard relayed. Phillip was seriously starting to dislike her.

"Does my mother know? Does she know where to visit?"

"No more questions" Jenny looked apologetically at Phillip with a hint of sympathy.

"You cannot do this!" he screamed at them the doorway shimmered slightly –

"No!" Phillip screamed and tried to put his hand on the seemingly open doorway – his arm went into a spasm and he was thrown to the other side of the room.

"I have heard 'men' have got a violent nature – you must understand this is precautionary." Jenny said.

"Answer me – Please!" Phillip pleaded with them.

"Your mother wishes to move on – whilst you're still around she cannot and will not be promoted" Jenny answered him reluctantly.

"Four minutes." The other guard said. Then they both disappeared to the other end of the corridor.

Phillip sat in shock huddled in the corner of his room, tears rolling down his cheeks. He didn't understand, his mother was talking only here last week, yes and she was a bit jumpy, but she didn't mention she didn't want to see him anymore.

He hauled himself up from the floor, he had carefully packed his discs and a soft toy his mother had given him, he didn't have long but he didn't really have any personnel belongings to speak of.

"X1250246."

"I'm ready" Phillip answered. His face flushed from the emotional turmoil. His stomach was endeavouring to do gymnastics as he waited.

"This way" the electromagnetic door disappeared and Phillip followed the guards. The thought of running didn't occur to him, all he had known was within these walls. Anyway, if he did they would terminate him.

They reached their destination- a containment room on the other side of the complex. He had been here once before – on arrival vague memories fleeted through his mind. The room was pink (apparently calming) no chairs just people standing waiting, what for only the selected few knew. Waiting for Phillip was another transfer and two Praeposter's – both he knew.

"This is the transfer you specified" Jenny talked to the older monitor. The other man being transferred was Christopher, Phillip looked questionably, Christopher he looked as bemused as Phillip felt. Phillip turned to face the Praeposter's, he didn't notice who they were when he first walked into the room. Phillips emotions had taken over his senses. The shock of his mother disowning him stopped him recognising Erin and Natasha.

"Two good specimens" Natasha commented lifting an eyebrow "Numbers correct." She turned to the guards they both nodded, evidently from the guards' faces neither liked nor dared to answer her. Phillip was amazed, why them specifically, he knew Erin hated Natasha. Erin stood slightly behind Natasha; her expression was wide-eyed, trying to tell him something. He surmised he was not supposed to recognize her. What favours had Erin and his mother done for him? Both were always too scared too embarrassed, not to hinder their precious careers. His thought turned to Natasha, she was in her element, power was something she always craved – Phillip felt suddenly out of his depth.

Erin and Natasha led the transfers to the hovercraft waiting for them on the grounds of the enclosure. The guards waited until they were on their way. Erin plotted in their coordinates into the on board computer – no one spoke, no one thought it necessary, each contemplating what was happening.

They pulled alongside the headquarters.

"What are we doing here?" Natasha asked Erin. "This is highly irregular!" Natasha was suspicious just as Erin had suspected.

"It's all right – Faith is to meet me towards the Pennies, it'll be fine." Erin replied.

"That group of islands are renowned for the trouble they cause with manoeuvres." Natasha was playing for time. Erin pulled a syringe from a compartment under the head up display. Natasha's eyes widened.

"I see you will be fine ma'am." Neither the men saw what Erin held in her hand as they had their backs towards her.

"Lie on your fronts" Natasha commanded.

"Why?" Christopher was alarmed. "We have never done this before on a transfer." Phillip suspected nothing having stayed at the Mendip enclosure all his life; he was already missing his friends.

"Don't ask questions," Natasha snapped.

"It's all right Natasha" Erin over ruling her and soothing the situation "we have had recent bouts of disturbance in the north; it's for your own safety. You wouldn't want to be someone's pet now would you V3642194?" Christopher and Phillip both did as they were instructed. Erin nodded to Natasha passing her a syringe. Natasha waiting for Erin's command looking at her superior. Erin nodded her head once – both women injected the men in their thighs simultaneously.

"What are you d...." Phillip tried to ask as everything went black.

"I told you I would not have a problem." Erin smiled at Natasha, keeping the dislike out of her voice. Not giving Natasha time to reply. "This isn't strictly protocol but I need you on a different assignment, as you know we have had various problems with guards I need you to accompany Jules to the highlands. It will be good experience as you're new to this department."

"But I have another gathering this weekend I was hoping you'd let me 'borrow' these two to entertain them." Natasha hoped to use them to pressure Erin into a mistake.

"I realise there will be some disappointment but I

have already been in contact with the pyramid. This is top priority, you understand this has to be controlled as soon as possible, you know there is an election coming soon." Erin had enough of explaining to Natasha she was far more tolerant of her than most, and this had to go smoothly.

"Divert any difficulties to other enclosures as a temporary measure and I will deal with the guards as soon as this transfer has been completed. I know you will support me in this as we are extremely under staffed at the moment. No one wishes to join the department anymore as the holidays have been cut so badly. I don't need to explain further do I Natasha?" Natasha wanted to ask more questions, her mind was awash with questions but now was not the right time.

"Have a report back by 18.00 tomorrow" Erin gave her a command that she would not misinterpret.

"Yes Ma'am." Natasha smiled she was not convinced but she neither had any proof or satisfactory evidence to what Erin's connection was with Phillip. Natasha left the vessel and headed towards headquarters where Jules was waiting for her with another craft. Erin smiled to herself, Jules and Natasha never got on and Jules would complete everything by the book. Erin put the new coordinates into the computer she had to meet with Ceres and Maria.

"I thought you'd never get here" Ceres was concerned.

"Is he alright?" Maria had climbed into the hovercraft checking Phillip's forehead. Neither Erin nor Ceres bothered to consider her, both were preoccupied. Erin had got out of the vessel and was pulling packages with Ceres into the craft.

"Have you got everything?" Erin asked, "they will

be out for a while yet so we've still got time.

"I had some serious explaining to do at the institute for that" Ceres said pointing to the laser in Erin's hand, "but the other stuff I got in stages, no one noticed" Ceres replied. Erin placed the laser over Phillips left thigh. The smell of burnt skin pervaded around them. A small incision was made underneath the skin, Erin placed the homing device into Phillips blood stream. Within seconds the chip was activated.

"How do we know it's got it?" Maria asked "we can't see it can we?" Erin handed over the implements to Ceres and placed her hand on the Control Panel.

"Information." She commanded the computer. "We seem to have a problem with X1250246, do you receive any vitals?"

"No information received, any input?"

"Confirmed" Erin replied. "End of report" the holographic image disappeared. No one spoke, Maria sat and held her sons hand the first time in his life he was to have freedom.

"Could you pass me the glue stick" Erin asked to no one in particular.

Her voice strained slightly. She mopped the blood with a cloth and started to use the hot glue to join the incision back together. Erin was relieved.

"Let's get him off here," Erin commanded no one argued her authority. All three women lifted his body onto the ground surrounding them. The long grass hid Phillip and the boat from view.

"Did you get the other body?" Erin asked.

"Yes a bit of a struggle – what would we do without faulty furnaces." Ceres laughed to break the tension – she was almost hysterical.

"Can you give me a lift with this?" they walked through the grass to where a man was laying, he had not been dead long. He was of the same height as

Phillip and would achieve their aim nicely.

"I removed the chip as you asked" Ceres spoke to Erin.

"Don't you still have it?" She replied.

"Yes I put it in my PERSONAL COMPUTER case" she pulled up her sleeve revealing a watch like instrument she clicked the lid open and pressed the electromagnetic to retrieve the chip.

"Great." Erin replied taking it off her. They lugged the body onto Erin's hovercraft where Erin inserted Phillip's personal chip into the corpse. They looked at each other, both Christopher and the corpse were face down, Erin checked for Christopher's pulse – he was fine.

"I haven't got long – I'll wake Phillip before I go. Stage two complete I hope I can get away with this and then we're home and dry."

All three women walked over to Phillip.

Phillip felt groggy, he could hear whispers, and sense unfamiliar smells around him which were invading his nose – trees, pine. Then, a strong smell of salt pervaded around him – sea? He remembered this smell from his childhood. His limbs felt heavy he still couldn't open his eyes. He started to panic; he tried to concentrate on what did work.

Another familiar smell wafted over him, the corner of Phillip's mouth twitched still unable to speak, it was a semblance of a smile, he knew he was safe, it was his mother.

"Do you think he's awake?" Phillip tried to talk but he could neither move nor speak so he lay their helpless whilst his mother discussed and worried over him.

"I'm not sure – if he doesn't wake soon we'll have a problem." Ceres as always was being very practical. "Have you seen the sky? The sun is starting to rise."

"Phillip" Maria gently shook his shoulder.

"Phillip!" Phillip could hear the panic in her voice but couldn't let her know he was all right. Well he thought he was alright. He tried to move his toes, start at the bottom work up, he kept telling himself. Suddenly he felt as if someone was sticking sharp implements in his feet. His thoughts were interrupted.

"Can I leave you two on your own?" Erin asked, "It's not far from here. I am not running off I need to be back at work or I will be missed?"

"You go – we'll be fine" Maria tried to be strong; she couldn't face the judge again. "It would be better to see if we've been caught out – you will be fine; but me and Ceres may have a problem when they put two and two together." Erin looked at her friends, if she had made a mistake they would be caught. If not they would all get away with it, she hoped that it was all going to be ok - she definitely didn't want to make a mistake now. Erin felt guilty about the others but she knew she had to go. It would be useful for them all for her to concentrate on checking her guards. Erin climbed back into the hovercraft waving at Maria and Ceres, hoping she could keep them all safe.

They both stood and watched Erin disappear into the distance the early morning mist from the sea engulfing her quickly. Phillip opened his eyes they were aching as if they had been shut for an eternity. He watched Ceres and his mother waving Erin goodbye. The saliva in his mouth-tasted metallic he rolled his tongue around his mouth the moisture dripped into his cracked lips reviving the pain. His hands felt for the dew-filled grass, gently he eased himself up, reaching out carefully Phillip managed to stand. Stiff as he was, he walked precariously over to his mother.

"Where do we go now?" His throat felt scratchy and hoarse. Ceres and Maria startled, initially doing nothing, but both of the women soon started to fuss. Phillip feeling suffocated snapped "You haven't answered my question?"

"Home" Maria answered "no one knows it exists, it was supposed to have been flooded years ago. Then again no one's really interested." She smiled "it's not that bad you know. Erin has had it as a safe house for years. One of Erin's favourites is there at the moment." Phillip gasped he thought he may as well go back to the enclosure now. "Don't worry she doesn't know who you are" he felt the thick band of stubble graze the back of his hand.

"I think this will be a giveaway." He looked into the water a smile touched the edge of his lips – he looked awful how he would pass for a woman? The oh so feminine qualities he had, being tall was not so much of a problem lots of the women that came to the enclosure were tall, it was his shape even the most muscular women weren't as broad across the chest as he was. He would have to wear loose fitting clothes to hide his anatomy.

"I don't know what you're worrying about" Ceres cut into his thoughts "not all women have large breasts, anyway I've solved that problem." She just smiled and had that look about her that one was not to ask questions. "Come on we've got to get you ready then out of here." Unceremoniously, Ceres jabbed him in the back.

"Do you really think the clothes we bought will be OK?" Maria wondered aloud.

"Yeah they'll be fine, come on Phillip" Ceres ordered, "I want to see you washed and clean." She patted the small pool of fresh water throwing him a bottle of cleansing fluid and a square piece of soft woven cloth.

"What's this for?" Phillip asked puzzled.

"Oh for God's sake – to dry yourself with." Ceres answered, trying not to laugh. Phillip embarrassed tried to explain his ignorance.

"I've never used this before – do I flap it to make the air dry off the water?"

"You rub it on your body it takes away the wet." Maria explained, giving Ceres a look to be quiet "Now hurry darling – we are running out of time I don't want any Praeposter's to stumble into us. We also have a long way to walk."

Phillip shrugged his shoulders and started to take off his clothes.

"Do you want some privacy – we can disappear you know" Ceres asked politely.

"I've never had that, so I'd prefer the company. I feel a bit exposed at the moment," he smiled. Maria started to unpack his clothes, methodically making sure for the last time he had the correct clothing. Worry was physically making Ceres sick. She tried to concentrate on her map, trying not to be obvious looking at Phillip; she had never seen a male naked before.

Her eyes kept veering from the map to Phillip. He took no notice of either of them, his body felt stiff, all his joints creaked and he had a chronic headache. He dipped his foot into the pool it was not as bad as he had expected it was warm. He slid into the pool tilting his head back letting the water soothe his aching body – floating he slowly let himself think of what had happened is this what it was like to be free? No one was watching him at any time – the reality of the situation seeped into his senses, he smiled for the first time properly in years, and his body was rejuvenated. The water washed over him easing his mind as well as his body.

Ceres started to panic they had to be in the woods before daylight.

"Come on we have to move as soon as possible"

"Phillip I've got your clothes here we'll have to hurry" said Maria, catching the panic in Ceres' voice. Phillip quickly removed himself from the water, drying himself with the cloth.

"Are you dry?" said Maria forever concerned.

"Yep, I think so; although I still feel a bit damp" Maria passed him his clothes. "Get dressed and I'll do your hair." Phillip looked at the trousers, shirt, boots, socks, and a bra with wadding stitched into the inside. With the last item he gave a questioning look at his mother. Laughing, Maria shrugged her shoulders "We are trying to make you look like a different gender." He pulled his trousers over his legs and they were soft to his skin.

"What's this?" He said as he pulled at a leg.

"Silk now hurry up. Can you help?" Although he had seen footwear at the enclosure he had not worn it since he was a child. Sitting down on a dry rock Maria fastened his boots. She picked up the bra.

"Stick out your arms." Phillip knew when to do as he was told, he may not have lived with his mother since being five but she still took control whenever she was with him.

"OW! What's that?" He felt the back of his shoulder blade and felt stitches, the bra snagged at them as he pulled it over his shoulder.

"It was where your chip was" Maria tutted. "It will have to be dressed at the house, now do what I ask please. Maria sprayed his back to numb the pain.

"Phillip you must hurry" Ceres chipped into their conversation, as she packed their belongings together. Maria turned her son around to see how her work looked. She tied back his hair "It is nice when you shave you look presentable." Maria smiled.

"I don't think this is going to work." Phillip stated

148

as he looked at his reflection.

"For god sake boy not every female is as petite as your mother." Ceres exploded "Anyway I always thought you were a pretty man – it'll work."

"Who are you trying to convince, you or me?" Phillip laughed.

"Move" Ceres ordered him giving a smack on his back "we've got some serious walking to do."

"How far do we have to walk?" Phillip asked as they followed each other in single file. Ceres had the map, which Erin had marked the route on.

"Surely you know where you are going Mum," Phillip queried behind him to Maria.

"Yes, but I don't know the way without having a guide to direct us." Maria explained, "Erin knows, as this is the way they bring the people to the safe house and it would look odd if we did it any other way."

"Shut up or we may be picked up." Ceres exploded, Phillip and Maria did as they were told.

Phillip was fascinated about his surroundings his leg hurt as it rubbed on the material. He had never been out of the enclosure since a child. It was beautiful. Through the trees, he could see mountains in the distance they had a purple hue where the sun glinted off them. He had to watch where he walked, the thistles and trees scratched either his face or his legs. A couple of times he nearly walked into a branch. As they came out of the woods, they entered a field, he smiled broadly and the sheep barely looked up from their grazing.

"Is this safe?" He asked to no one in particular.

"Yes, but I want to be the other side before 08.30 just in case" Ceres left the sentence unfinished.

"Why?"

"Well Erin said the farm has a routine and it starts here around 09.00. I'd prefer to be gone before she gets here." Ceres seemed to pick up the pace, as did the others, none were too eager to be caught. Phillip returned to his sightseeing to keep his mind from worrying, the lake that the field led to, took all his attention. He watched as it lapped over the grass gently licking at the base of the few trees that separated it from the field. He could still see the mountains in the distance, he realized as he walked that the lake must follow the whole of the valley to the bottom edge of that first mountain. That would be a long way to walk, he smiled to himself at his own joke. He was used to passing time; he had lots of practice at the enclosure. He had often wondered what it would be like to roam around the countryside – not once had he expected to be able to. Vague memories from his childhood flashed into his mind running around a vineyard laughing with his mother – she had tickled him until he could laugh no longer. The sadness that was always in her eyes left briefly for that one moment. He treasured that memory, would he ever be able to laugh again or always just have to pretend?

Phillip didn't know how far they had walked, he hadn't noticed the sun beating on his back, cushioned by his memories they walked on.

"Would you like a drink?" Maria asked he broke out of his reverie.

"Yes, that would be great – thanks" taking a sip he looked at his surroundings, to his amazement they were by the range of mountains he had noticed earlier. "Where to now?" He asked.

"Through a small pass and there should be a boat awaiting us" Ceres answered whilst drinking her drink.

"No hover?" Phillip questioned.

"No we didn't want the noise, besides the computer would refer us back to the mainframe, I think the ancient system of a boat would help us to achieve our goal. Erin has kept it in good condition, I hope we find it as it's hidden in the undergrowth."

After a small break they got back on course – the mountains sheltered them from the heat and the walk through the pass was uneventful, but as Erin promised as they reached the end of the pass, they discovered the tied up boat.

"This is really strange how this pass goes nowhere" Ceres commented. The water edged its way up to the gully with no pathways extending from it. "I think it was flooded when the temperature changed. Must have been used hundreds of years ago" Maria mused trying to recall her history lessons. Ceres still kept charge and they gently rowed around the edge of the lake until they were in the cover of the trees. Checking her map "I think this is the shortest crossing it's going to get choppy now." The boat rocked slightly as the waves caressed the old wood. The land was getting closer, suddenly Ceres stopped, turned to Phillip, then looked pointedly at Maria.

"Oh, I suppose we are going to hear the ground rules," Maria said with some emphasis on "rules".

"Ok Phillip you know there is a woman on the island, her name is Faith, don't let her know who you are. She doesn't know your past just that you are to be kept a secret in the safe house, your name is Leah." Maria paused. "What I'm saying is she's trustworthy to a point – she is a monitor after all. Don't let her see you are a man, whatever the cost – It could be your life." With this, Maria did something she had wanted to do since he was a child. Maria gave him a hug and gently kissed his forehead. "Be safe" was all she said. Nodding to Ceres they gently made their way to the island that was to be Phillip's new home.

On the beach stood a young woman who was waving at them. She had blazing auburn hair that glinted in the sun.

Erin pulled the craft up to Lakeside.

"Computer – I have an incident to report."

"Incident log – open" the computer answered in the metallic not quite human voice.

"X1250246 – has had a heart attack in transportation" lasers ran over the body that had taken Phillip's place. The body that Ceres, Maria and Erin had carefully obtained for this purpose in Phillips place. Erin felt physically sick.

"Heart attack confirmed – chip shut down to commence."

"I will dispose of the body when I have delivered the other transfer – inform the guards I have arrived." Erin gave the order.

Two guards came towards her craft, Erin pulled out another file. She then injected Christopher to wake him.

"Take him, he'll seem confused – I'll dispose of the body" Erin ordered.

"Are you all right Ma'am? What happened?" The guards asked concerned for their superior.

"I'm fine he had a reaction to the aesthetic – heart attack" Erin paused feigning her concern. "I will head to the Institute now get him settled first." She said pointing to Christopher – Not yet fully conscious – Erin wanted to be gone before he awakened. The hard bit was done the enclosure had an Institute on the grounds Erin plotted the craft to take her there. Slowly she docked the craft against the wall of the building where a hole opened up.

"Computer release the body," Erin ordered. Slowly it rolled into the opening.

"Is the chip shut down complete?" Erin questioned.

"Yes – is the body to be disposed of?" It answered.

"Yes – now is fine" Erin said weariness creeping into her voice. The body dropped onto a metal ledge within the opening of the wall to make it ready for cremation.

"Complete" it confirmed. Erin put the co-ordinates for her home. With only her thoughts to accompany her, finished. She thought, after a moment's hesitation - No it is just the beginning.

18

As Phillip looked down at his now sun burnt skin as it glistened with perspiration, he wondered how did he get here? Yes, he wasn't a novice with women, but then again the women who "visited" him were bureaucrats, he was used as a toy. This was so very different and difficult, there wasn't any expectation of any affection; for God's sake, she didn't even know he was a man! God, how beautiful she is – Faith had burnished auburn hair which shone on the top of her head like a halo as it fell onto her golden skin sparkled in the sun. Mother where are you? The question screamed in his head – what was this feeling, he needed explanations now more than ever. He felt sick and weak at the knees other men at the enclosure had said about the feeling, what was it they had called it? Lust? The other men had favourites from the women who came to use their bodies to fulfil their needs that had followed them around daily. Phillip thought about the women that visited him, yes, he had his favourites but he could still control his brain. Yes, they did things to him which were by no mistake pleasurable and enabled him to 'perform' to please, yes that's what they had called it." Faith turned around and looked at him.

"What's the matter, Leah?"

"Oh I'm sorry I was daydreaming" Phillip replied he still hadn't gotten used to people calling him by that name. "Do you want to go for a drink back at the house? I think we've managed to finish what we needed to achieve today."

They went inside Phillip's house, although technically it was his mother's friend. It leaned slightly to one side but it was five hundred years old. Faith was initially amazed to find the stainless steel sink in the kitchen.

"Where's the water purifier she was rummaging in the kitchen cupboards?"

"I use the taps. I find it quicker" Phillip replied.

"What!"

"The taps?" He went over to the sink and turned on the tap until crystal water came out.

"That is amazing – you would be surprised how advanced they were in the 21st century" Faith carried on "I always thought they were barbarians- all those wars were ridiculous when you look back on them. Don't you find it time consuming getting a drinking vessel and everything?"

"I never thought about it," Phillip said shrugging his shoulders. "Mmm I like the quirks of the old place not all that sterile cleanliness." Phillip's thoughts were wondering from the conversation, he could hardly breathe this close to Faith, he had no other friends, keeping his own company especially as he was disguised as a woman. Life in the outside world was just too difficult to have friends. Faith was different.

Faith took a sip of water walking back outside and enjoying the view over the ocean beyond. The waves lapped onto the beach in the distance. Phillip silently walked up behind her disturbing her thoughts. She jumped slightly spilling her water

"Oh you gave me a shock." Faith laughed at herself. "I was just thinking how lucky we are being here – I'm pleased I was sent out here as a farm hand. Don't look so sceptical, yes better than being cramped on the mainland"

"Don't you want to go back?" Phillip asked. "I would have thought this place would have been a demotion especially having worked already on the mainland." Faith smiled at him.

"No, I prefer the company here" she replied. They

lapsed into comfortable silence between them as they enjoyed each other's company as they had done for many nights previously. Phillip tried to control his thoughts – looking at Faith stirred something inside that made him feel helpless, Faith saw the way he looked at her every night.

"Why do you look at me in that way?" she asked. "Others have looked at me in that way before." Her voice was gentle, probing, even tones.

"Oh – I'm sorry didn't mean to upset you." Phillip said, horrified – He had heard that some women preferred to be with other women – not going to the enclosure.

"Do you like other women?" He asked, realising that is what she thought he was.

"What on earth gave you that idea?" Phillip felt as if she had physically slapped him in the face. Faith was horrified – she didn't want to lose a friend over her sexual preferences. She was confused yes, she was attracted to Leah but never before had she liked others like her. On the mainland, friends had told her to visit the enclosures to relieve herself. The thought of being in the same room as others having sex appalled her or even worse the 'parties' she had heard about – it made her feel creepy just thinking about it. She knew her friends went to each other's homes and participated in watching each other while they participate in sexual activities. They used to laugh and call her a prude when she refused to join in.

When she was in classes at school she loved reading about old traditions, she was amazed that people got married, weird concept ugh. She thought about them constantly living with one of those animals in the enclosures, although it must have been nice being that close to someone whether they were male or female. It might have been like what she and Leah had together.

Phillip's brain and stomach simultaneously spun as he watched Faith stare out to the sea. He didn't know how to tell, or if he should tell her – he needed to tell her but how – how would she accept him, it was so alien to her?

"Come and sit beside me Leah – You are so tall I have to strain my neck when I look at you," Faith asked, to ease the tension she had obviously caused, Phillip sat on the parched grass next to her. His skin tingled as he felt her close proximity. Faith turned towards him and stared into Phillips eyes, they were nearly as blue as the Atlantic – they glistened, the same as the sea when the sun rose at dawn, Phillip felt uncomfortable her green eyes pierced into his sole. He had too many secrets for her to do that, he couldn't look away. Her hand gently brushed against his cheek feeling the contours of his face. Her tiny hands sent sparks through Phillips body. Shutting his eyes, thoughts ran through his brain.

"Why now – I cannot cope with this."

"Who are you Leah?" Faith's question hit him. Phillips eyes shot open – he felt sick. Recovering his composure he smiled to hide his emotions.

"What do you mean?" He answered.

"Do…Do you like looking at other women, do you go to the enclosures?" Faith was wary of asking such a probing question. Phillip just laughed heartily – Faith wished she had never mentioned it. Seeing the look of dejection on her face, Phillip pulled himself together – not answering her question, he asked her one instead.

"Have you been to the enclosures?" He collected himself enough to ask.

"Never" Faith answered, "I don't like the idea of being in a room on my own with a man it scares me." Faith carried on, "I heard they were like caged animals."

157

"If only you knew" Phillip smiled "would you mind if we had a cuddle?" He asked tentatively.

"No not at all" She replied not looking at him, she carried on "I am attracted to you, it's never happened before, I always thought I preferred men, well the idea of them anyway – I suppose I have surprised myself." She tucked herself inside Phillips shoulder. "Wow, you are flat chested – never noticed before. It must be so much easier to work with. Mine keeps getting in the way." Faith said as she pumped up her already large breasts. Phillip couldn't concentrate when she did things like that. He smelt her hair ripe cornfields filled his nostrils. Putting his fingers through her soft hair, curling it around his fingers. Faith moved her face towards his; tentatively kissing his lips, – they became increasingly urgent – her hands ran through his black hair. Shivers ran through their bodies the urgency of the moment taking over both of their minds.

Faith slid her hand inside his tunic. Panic, confusion, and fear gripped Phillip and he pulled away gasping for breath. Faith looking for the question in his eyes.

"What's the matter – have I done something I shouldn't have?" Phillip just shook his head not daring to speak. Faith spoke trying to ease the tension and to ease the confusion within herself. "Look I've never been to bed with anyone before either." Faith was scared "I'm not sure what to do – only to myself. Do you want to join me?" Phillip felt like a rabbit in the headlights wanting to answer 'yes', but knowing he would blow his own cover the moment he did. Instead, he chewed his lip. Faith took the look on his face as a yes. Slowly she started to undress, her hands moved over her soft skin, taking off her clothes one by one. Phillip couldn't tell her to stop, he didn't want her to. Knowing if she found out what he was – he would have to go back to the enclosure – it could be a trap – she could be a monitor. Silently he cried in his mind. "What am I to do?"

Faith placed her clothes on the cracked earth. Gently standing on her toes, she kissed his lips, Phillips eyes were everywhere taking in every inch of her body.

"I've never done this before with anyone watching, at first I was scared but I feel calm now." Faith uttered, hardly audible. Staring at Phillip her hand went to her mouth, with her tongue, she wet her lips and her forefinger slowly moved around her mouth. Slowly her hand moved down her body leaving a glistening streak of water between her breasts and down to her stomach. Phillip stood transfixed hardly daring to breathe. Faith moved slowly to the ground opening her legs, she gently ran her finger through the soft down of her pubic hair feeling for the moistness within. Slowly she moved her hips back and forth her body stating to feel weak from the pleasure. Phillip stood watching wanting to be part of her but not daring. Faith's breathing became heavy and with her, other hand she again put her forefinger in her mouth. She then gently traced the contours of her breasts feeling her body as the pace of her hips quickened her head moved back shutting her eyes in pleasure. Phillip got down on his knees and whispered.

"This is who I am." She turned to see him taking off his clothes, still not spent; she stopped abruptly as she saw his bare white chest. Fear gripped her, as she lay motionless whilst he undid his trouser cord slowly revealing his own identity. Faith couldn't believe her own eyes seeing him naked – she couldn't breathe. Her mind flipped back to all their conversations and of the rumours she had heard from the enclosure. She lay still from shock and fear, she was all eyes and totally rigid. Phillip's hand stroked her body feeling every crevice, wanting to ease her shock.

"I won't hurt you, no matter what you've heard." Phillip said trying to allay her fears "Don't go away, I think I love you." Faiths body felt on fire, everywhere he touched. His hand moved down between her thighs with the palm of his hand stroked her already wet pubic hair; steadily he found what he was looking for. He edged his fingers into her vagina. Faith gasped in pleasure not believing what was happening to her – she didn't care, as she had never had another person feel her skin. Prickly sensations ran down her body Phillip slowly edged deeper with his finger moving slightly so he could kiss her gently. Her instincts had taken over gently probing into his mouth so tenderly not quite sure what to do he moved slowly down her body circling her breasts with his tongue following the trails she had left herself towards her abdomen. Faiths body started to burn her feet were on fire and it was creeping towards her abdomen. Nudging her legs apart with his head slowly he licked her it rasped across her hair; he parted her with his tongue. Her breathing became a heavy pant; she achieved a climax quicker than she had ever been able to achieve on her own. Phillip slid inside her as so not to hurt her, rocking slightly and kissing her body all over. The passion took over both of them; their bodies entwined becoming one; kissing each other urgently not able to get each other's tastes quick enough. Phillip forgot to take things slowly as the moment overtook his senses breathing heavily they both climaxed. Phillip fell on top of her with exhaustion and relief – good or bad, he didn't have to hide anymore.

Faith recovering her composure and to her astonishment found his penis. After stroking him, she pulled herself onto her elbow.

"So who are you?"

160

19

"Erin" Faith's face came through on Erin's computer; it was the most secure way of contacting her.

"Hi" Erin replied, she loved hearing how Phillip was, he was family. She had known him since he was born. Blocking it from her mind trying to be professional she concentrated on the situation at hand. Her smile faded, Faith reported regularly but today she was agitated. "Everything alright?"

"I'm pregnant" Faith blurted out, she had hoped to tell her slightly better than that, she didn't have the time, Phillip would be back soon from harvesting – it had happened early this year. Erin felt ice run down her spine – the warm blood drained from her head to her toes.

"How far?" Erin needed facts; she could deal in facts not what ifs.

"I think around six weeks" Faith paused "It's been more often than I would care to tell you."

"You've not been to any enclosures?" Erin hoped, although she felt she was treating Faith with disrespect, she knew the answer, and she was going to kill Phillip he was supposed to be under cover. Faith should have known better, on the other hand, he had been indoctrinated to appease and to keep women happy, the research she had done over the years had been informative, she found men had a physical need. Personally, she didn't understand the feeling. An old saying crossed her mind 'what you don't have you don't miss.' Her conscience got the better of her, she had been back to the enclosure, her guilt at the treatment of specimens under her own jurisdiction disgusted her, and she was taking out her frustration on Faith.

"Stay where you are, I can get this sorted." Erin became her usual bossy self once the shock had worn off.

"I'm not having an abortion," Faith stubbornly cut into her thoughts. Erin could see her physically bristle, she had not answered some of her questions but that was what Erin had trained her for. She had trained her well. This didn't stop her exploding at Faith, it was exactly what she wanted to do.

"For crying out loud, it's not registered, you know the risk and what's been hidden for years, and it could be a boy. I take it, it has been conceived naturally, what were you thinking? I don't know if I can get around this." Erin paused her body was losing control of its internal thermometer; her anger was literally making her body leak with sweat.

"You've managed to lose a certain person, surely you can register this?" Faith patted her stomach and was angry, she needed her help, not her condemnation. She had always had a quick temper but the conversation ended as the connection was severed. They could sort it out now, it was as much their fault as it was hers they had thrown them together, and it had always been their secret, now it was Faith's too.

As the connection went dead, Erin was blaming herself, not knowing what to do. Faith was put there under a misconception – it is a conception all right. She had not told Phillip what would happen, turning to look out of her window to the beach, she needed to cool down, this would never do. If she had the time she would go to the medical institute for an injection, it was ridiculous at her age to suffer these sweats. Other women had gone through it but it was affecting her judgement.

"Computer, contact Maria Stevenson and Ceres Zanuti - a secure line" they all needed to sort this out.

The way her hormones were, she didn't trust herself.

The three friends met in the orange grove north of the conurbation. It was a particularly quiet area away from the centre and the pyramid.

"How far gone is she?" Maria asked, she had expected something to go wrong it had all been too easy: the escape, his death, the cremation everything. Natasha's knowledge worried them all she knew bits of information they were sure, what she really knew none of the three couldn't quite figure out.

"Six weeks – and she will not terminate it. I couldn't get it done very quickly, so many others who visit the enclosures regularly go to a private clinic." Erin stated, annoyed more at herself for the mishandling of the situation. "I could have said she visited an enclosure. In fact she'll have too – someone else must have got caught." Erin stopped mid flow of her sentence.

"What's wrong?" Ceres asked.

"Do you remember Natasha's party?" Erin turned to Maria, ignoring Ceres.

"I'd prefer not to." Maria scrunched her face as a child would when they had eaten something horrible.

"Anyway," Erin continued, dismissing her friend. "The woman – what was her name? Grrr, I can't remember, well she has a young daughter, I'm not a hundred percent on this, but surely she is too old for daughter that age?" Erin blew out her breath talking mainly to herself, Maria and Ceres just looked askance at her, neither knew what she was talking about. Nevertheless, neither wanted to stop her train of thought.

"Sabrina, that was it, she must be about forty, there's no way she should have a ten year old not via the lottery anyway." Erin turned to Maria "You've got to talk to Faith; she's got to have sex with someone, anyone in the enclosures."

"What!" Maria and Ceres said simultaneously.

"It's tough if Phillip doesn't like it, we are saving his life and ours." Erin paused not letting either friend answer her. "It took Ceres and me years to stop the pyramid from stalking our every move; all three of us have given up too much to risk everything now."

"I don't think this will work" Maria said "I only meant that time we took Phillip to the old house – she will not do it, she is very moralistic, that warned me constantly, I thought she would report us all."

"She hasn't any choice," "She's also not speaking to me either – she refuses any contact when I try" Erin, said. "Can you go and see them?" Erin turned to Maria.

"Of course, any excuse to see my son" she smiled "I know we have a slight crisis going on but" Maria paused for effect "Do you realise I'm going to be a grandmother" Maria laughed, "I always craved a family." Erin and Ceres looked at their friend astonished at her thought process.

"I will never understand how your brain works." Ceres said shaking her head but laughing at the same time.

"What do you want me to do? – I don't think I am going to be of any use." Ceres said.

"I need your help finding Sabrina; I need facts and figures before we do anything." Erin winced she knew she would probably be caught, she changed her mind.

"No, I'll do it through the bureau, risky due to Natasha but, I'll put Sabrina under investigation, I'm sure she's my level so Natasha would not have security clearance, I just hope she doesn't know too much. I don't know why nothing has been done so far. I will deal with her and if she is in my department, I can watch her. I want to know what she wants from me."

Erin stood up "I'll send a communication to you both later today." She looked over to Maria "When are you leaving?"

"I'll go now, I pretended I'm sick" Maria smiled "here we go again, one of these days, life will be easy. Good Luck" with that, hugging each other and with regret they dispersed to complete each task alone.

"I thought Erin would have come" Faith uttered in disbelief at Maria as she walked into the safe house.

"Does he know yet?" Maria asked. Phillip was out in the sunshine picking the vines.

"No" Faith said shaking her head "you should have told me his gender. I started to think I was going mad."

"I'm sorry it was for your own safety to avoid any indiscretions. It's too late now; we didn't know how we could trust you." Maria said emotionless.

"For God's sake" Faith muttered at her, so Phillip would not hear them "I should have known he is your son."

"Why?"

"Why don't you care, you come here telling me what to do – under orders from Erin?" Sarcasm dripped from Faith. "What have you come for?"

"I'm to take you to an enclosure. I can't go in, but you can, you are a monitor and we need the liaison recorded." Maria paused; "Do you want to keep this child or not?"Faith nodded, lost for words.

This stupid headstrong girl would kill him. What for? What morals were left?

Faith felt upset. "Don't shout at me until you know what you are talking about. I won't listen until then."
"Do as you are told." Maria spoke in a whisper, Faith knew she was only venting her own stupidity on Maria, but she never showed emotion. She didn't understand.

"Faith, my dear girl, I have protected my son as best I can all his life, away from the city when he was little, I love him more than anything" Maria smiled "Is this a physical or emotional attachment you both have?"

"I love him" Faith looking to the floor felt like a chastised child.

"Good and I'm going to be a grandmother," Maria laughed "Come here you daft girl; embracing her in a bear hug, she couldn't have any distance between them.

"When do we go?" Faith asked, as would a subdued child.

"Tonight, you tell Phillip, I presume you know who he is now?" Maria stated.

"Yes"

"Good, therefore you know the risk you have taken" Maria stated. "So we have to get you there now. I am going to wait here, go and tell Phillip what you want. I don't care; we have to make sure they won't check the DNA of this baby." Maria didn't want to alarm her, they could have a problem, she could have a boy to keep safe, the consequences of that particular scenario wasn't worth thinking about, with the all the information they had stored in that dark room."

"Put a smile on your face and use all your training, you are going to have to lie." Maria didn't wish to hurt her son.

"I don't know how to tell him, you." Faith cried.

"I am doing a favour for Erin and taking you with me. Just keep it simple and go!" Faith did as she was told and disappeared through the door.

Maria wandered around the room touching objects that were familiar; their home. Her life, her past, now Phillip and Faith's future. A web of lies that kept growing.

She didn't want to explore that, she had made a pact with herself in a cell years ago. She was going to find more strength from somewhere. She not only had her son to protect now, but his family.

As Maria stared out of the window, she saw her son walking up the hill to the house. He had discarded his disguise as there was no one else on the island. Phillip stood tall gently holding Faith's small hand. Something hurt Maria inside; everyone should be allowed the happiness that shone from their faces. No one should be repressed, she smiled to herself, wasn't it this sort of thinking that got her into this mess in the first place?

"Mum." Phillip came running over and gave her a hug as he had always done when she was allowed to visit him at the enclosure. These visits had drained both of them, this time it was different. "Has Faith told you she is coming with me?" Maria asked. "Yes, but don't keep her away too long." As he gave her a gentle squeeze.

"Ah, I see that you have got to know each other more than I expected." Faith shook her head slightly and stared intently at Maria. Maria didn't acknowledge Faith, but understood she had not told him, he didn't know. It wasn't mentioned.

"I hear your talents have now progressed to cooking," she laughed with her son.

"I think Faith may have been exaggerating but I try." Phillip had slowly learnt to attempt sarcasm.

"You cook, and we will see, Faith and I will pack she needs to go today." Maria smiled. "Yes Mum, God I feel five again – isn't it great." As he ran into the kitchen pulling out fresh vegetables from the basket.

Maria went with Faith to pack – she was not sure how long this was going to take.

Communication J6491 – flashed onto Ceres' communicator, she loved getting messages from the Praeposter's, who else added a number to their communications. She knew this was from Erin, this time she had made it official it was Erin who was taking the risk. She was not sure this was entirely safe; taking a drink from her cup, she placed her finger on the print decoder immediately the message came on to her personal screen.

Sabrina Johnston – Agricultural minister – Home Address

Ceres spat out the milk all over the desk

"Are you OK?" Debbie, (who sat next to her), inquired.

"Yeh I'm fine" Ceres answered, trying to wipe it off the screen and decoder – frantically.

"Are you sure, you are really pale, in fact you're slightly green" Debbie laughed at her own joke.

"Honestly I'm OK, the drink just went down the wrong way."

"Just checking" Debbie answered and carried on with her own work. Ceres thought Erin had totally lost any ounce of integrity she had ever possessed. She didn't dare contact her personally; she quickly downloaded the information to Erin's computer, bypassing the messages team.

"Do you know Debbie; I don't feel too well I think you are right, I should go home."

"I will see you in the next shift then. Go and get some sleep." Debbie whispered as Ceres trying not to be rude smiled and rushed out of the complex.

Immediately she was in the square outside, she snapped at her communicator.

"Erin Holt"

"Hi, thanks," Erin said.

"Are you insane that is a high ranking member – what are you going to do visit her at home?" Ceres' sarcastic attitude was whizzing across the airwaves, into Erin's office. Erin smiled she was going to have apoplexy when she knew the truth.

"Of course, I told you I knew her, she was at Natasha's party. I've met her through work as well." Erin didn't pause she knew Ceres' temper would not let her listen if she inhaled one breath.

"I'm going home you are going to risk everything – the games up." Ceres was not amused by Erin's scheme.

"Don't over dramatise the situation, go home and have a drink of that illegal coffee you are so addicted too. It just may calm you down." Erin cut off the communication leaving Ceres in the middle of square, stunned and for the first time in her own memory totally speechless.

20

Erin sat starring into space she knew Ceres would calm down; she also knew she was right. She was dreading approaching Sabrina, what Ceres didn't know was she was renowned for being a complete bitch; if she so much suggested she had broken the rules... Erin wiped the thought from her mind – she had to be positive.

Erin spoke aloud practising how she was going to approach this woman, who she barely knew.

"Hi, Sabrina – have you been to any of Natasha's parties recently?" No, she knew that was the wrong way to approach her.

"Sabrina, its Erin Holt here." That was better. "Would you mind if I come over to discuss a difficulty I've come across?" God she would tear her apart.

"Sabrina, Erin here could we meet soon?" No. There was a knock at the door – it was Natasha.

"Hi, Erin." She sat down in front of Erin as if she was an old acquaintance. Erin didn't feel the same way.

"Can I help you?" Erin asked, her eyebrow raised slightly, her whole body oozed with dislike. It didn't matter how well Natasha was liked by the other members of the pyramid – Erin was not so sure. She could never quite define why? A memory, she doubted herself – a natural dislike – possibly. Natasha was sure. She assumed everyone would like her – most did. She personally just hated her with no apparent reason; Erin grated at Natasha's false veneer. No one at work would affect her as she had.

"Did I hear you mention Sabrina? I can contact her if you wish. Natasha smiled she was not sure about Erin everyone said she was very professional; she certainly never let anyone in. She was not even interested at her party. Maybe she had a relationship with Maria. Why Sabrina? It must be work as she had seen the video footage with Phillip – a disgrace the Enclosures should be punished for letting an absolute beautiful specimen such as him go and die.

Erin was annoyed about this; she didn't think anyone had heard her. She felt sick about contacting Sabrina anyway.

"I don't think it would follow procedure, asking a subordinate to contact a senior ranking official" Erin stated, Natasha was unperturbed.

"Its fine, I wanted to ask you what you were going to do about the enclosures. I'm sure you know about Phillip" Natasha paused.

"I'm sorry I only know them by number" Erin cut in, her stomach was working its way through her ribcage.

'Oh, I'm sorry – Phillip, the young man I used for the main event, at my party.' Natasha knew Erin was hiding something – it had to do with Maria.

Natasha wanted her reaction, if what her mother used to mumble in the asylum had any semblance of truth in it–it was vague at the moment, but Natasha thought she was on to something. Hadn't she pulled a lot of favours just to get close to this woman? She knew as much now as she did then. A smiled etched its way onto the corner of her mouth - the footage.

"I thought you knew him" Natasha stopped abruptly, her face a mask of innocence. "You know what good terms I'm with the guards – he was one of my favourites. I thought he was one of yours." Natasha paused to see the effect – Erin's face showed nothing other than bewilderment, although she didn't dare to use her vocal cords, they seemed to have seized, she just shrugged not trusting herself to speak.

"The security said that you had cornered him for

yourself. Such a pity that you pulled rank like that. I asked the guards – he was very good. I don't blame you – particularly well trained, I can take most of the credit for that myself." Erin couldn't take anymore.

"Oh yes X1250246, and your point is? I'm allowed to use my position occasionally. I'm sure you understand." Erin smiled.

"What! You haven't heard? It's a disgrace. I've been keeping a close eye on him – you must admit he was good." Natasha mused, she was not at all side tracked, and she just needed Erin to think she was. "I was generally hoping you would get bored – I wasn't going to let anyone else sneak him from under my nose. Anyway, as he had been transferred and I presumed you weren't interested, I went to find him. I don't wish to upset you but he died in admission. Like I said it was a bloody disgrace." Natasha waited for a reaction on Erin's face; she was disappointed she thought she would break. She licked her lips in anticipation, she would get a reaction. "So what are we going to do about it? I thought I would investigate, it is a complete debacle." Erin looked into Natasha's eyes she couldn't read a thing.

"I don't think it was a suspicious death, it would have been reported to me as you know I took him myself and he was healthy when I left him." Erin unconsciously ran the back of her hand across her brow "It is such a shame I haven't been to that enclosure recently."

"I am sorry – never mind, I am sure I can train a new pet for your pleasure." Natasha stood up, she turned before leaving.

"I hope you can come to another one of my parties, I was wondering, whether to host one in remembrance of Phillip. Would you mind if I could have the footage of you and Phillip?" Erin was feeling physically abused.

"I think you will find there is none I tend not to have voyeuristic tendencies like yourself." Erin added, but she couldn't think of anything else to say. Natasha took no notice of Erin's comment, she had no idea of her inner turmoil and as an afterthought, she added.

"If you like, you can bring Maria – as a personal tribute. I thought we would invite a few from the office. How about Faith?" Natasha never waited for an answer she just walked out, Erin always used Faith for the best jobs, and she was jealous, she had no idea how close to the truth she was.

If Erin was previously nervous about Sabrina – it was nothing to how she felt now – neither knew. First deal with Sabrina then Natasha. Erin needed to leave work, she grabbed together her belongings, and headed for Sabrina's home. On her way she tried to regain her composure and knew she would have to be fully compass mentis when she faced Sabrina.

21

"Can I help?" the disconnected voice came through the interface.

"I'm from the pyramid, I was told by Natasha it would be Ok to visit" Maria tried to sound as if she belonged there.

"Please come in, we have had a few new ones recently." Maria and Faith walked into the waiting room. The guard was pleasant and she smiled indulgently at them both.

"Do I know you?" She turned to Maria.

"I don't think so, we may have met outside of here" Maria mentally kicked herself, that was far too obvious; she would have to be more careful.

"You just look familiar" the guard looked puzzled as if trying to recall something. Maria knew her all right, she used to guard the room when she visited Phillip. "Not to worry," the guard physically shrugged her shoulders. "Do you have any preferences? Mind you be careful with them, we lent one to Natasha and her cronies before and they wore him out" the guard made a guttural noise that Maria and Faith presumed was a laugh. "Had a bloody heart attack." Faith felt the muscles in her legs give way and promptly found something to lean on.

"Not to worry, we're first timers." Maria smiled.

"It is such a shame you have just missed Natasha – she's keeping them busy at the moment" Maria was relieved; they could have ruined everything by being slightly earlier.

"I had better stop chatting and get them, any preferences – blonde or dark?"

"Any" Maria smiled at Faith; her face had drained of any colour.

Actually if you are busy I will let my colleague go in on her own" Maria smiled, "I feel slightly too old for this sort of thing" Smiling with an effort she didn't think possible, she glanced at Faith. Maria didn't know if Faith could go through with this, she was afraid for her as she had no other choice.

The glass, which surrounded Erin, felt claustrophobic, even though she could see over the conurbation in which she had lived for most of her life. She clung to the back of the lift. Erin hated heights, everyone kept telling her to see a hypnotherapist – she laughed at the thought, she had too many secrets to let the pyramid into her brain. Just imagine if they probed, which she was certain they would. Heights or to be hypnotised? Oh well, she would have to put up with the fear, jolted out of her reverie the lift shuddered to a stop.

Erin, renowned herself for being inflexible within the pyramid she dreaded facing Sabrina, until Natasha's party she never thought her as someone who would break the rules. Now she needed her help. The glass door opened smoothly leaving Erin with the same nervous anticipation of when she took her exams at college. Pull yourself together you are not eighteen now! Erin cursed herself, she rarely felt any moment of self-doubt. Banishing all negative thoughts, she physically pulled herself straight, fixed a smile on her face and walked into the space beyond.

"Erin darling" Sabrina smiled, her well-groomed appearance from beyond Erin's eye line.

"Hello Sabrina how's the ministry?"

"You know all things considered – we have just celebrated our crop of Oaks – we were not sure they would survive" Sabrina waved her arm dramatically towards the day beds. "Excuse my manners, please come and sit down." Erin was surprised to see bedding piled onto the edges. Sabrina followed her gaze.

"Sorry about the mess, I seem to permanently have girls here. All Angel's friends seem to congregate here" Sabrina paused "so what can I help you with? You don't usually make house calls?"

"I have actually come for some advice, I realise I'm being presumptuous, you are the only person I could think of to ask." Erin knew she was not getting to the point but now she was here she was stumbling over her words.

"Now, now Erin this must be important for you not to get to the point." Sabrina laughed at Erin's squirming, although she had not worked with her directly on many occasions, Erin's reputation had also preceded her. Erin knew this was her one and only chance, if she failed she couldn't see another option. It was not the first time she had been in this position.

"I'm sorry – this is a new to me" she smiled at Sabrina knowing she could turn any time from the pleasant woman into a harridan. "Anyway, I've got a slight problem with a young girl who works for me. Very trustworthy and to be honest could turn into one of my best operatives."

"Go on" Sabrina cut in.

"Well, she seems to have been influenced by another member in my department, visiting the enclosures. So let's say she's now won the lottery but she's two years two young." Erin finished relieved.

"God is that all" Sabrina smirked at Erin's discomfort with the situation. "I take it she has suddenly become protective over it – will not go to the institute etc."

"Exactly" Erin said.

"God woman, it happens all the time. As you have obviously guessed, I'm no exception. I take it that is why you have come to me?" Sabrina turned to Erin staring at her fully. "You know you shouldn't be such a prude – I'd have lost half of my department when Natasha worked for me. She tends to have that affect on people."

"What do I do?" Erin asked.

"You can't do anything. I can though, the lottery shall be fixed, and we tend to have computer viruses from time to time." Sabrina's grin became slightly sinister. "Every time the respected elite find themselves in a dilemma." Sabrina suddenly became very businesslike. "I'll be in my office tomorrow – I have the security to pass it. I need names and we will get her checked out. She had better pray it's a girl or she will have to go to the institute after all." Erin understood, this was her dismissal.

Erin walked along the traverse, looking over the docklands area – she had heard of religions in old history lessons, not that anyone believed in that now, it just wasn't scientifically sound. However, if there was something she prayed – let it be a girl.

Part Three

Eva

22

The numbers flickered on the wall – the rations. Eva hated her job it was so depressing. She shifted uncomfortably in her chair, rubbing her eyes to remove the sweat that dribbled into them. The temperature regulating system was working but she found it unbearable. Unsteadily, she moved the lower part of her back against the lumber of her chair. The different types of pain she was getting now were excruciating, and this was normal! Eva gently rubbed her extended stomach in a circular motion, for months now she tried to ignore this and pretend her nightmare had never happened. Other women thought it was an honour to be picked – she didn't. When her order came through she had begged and pleaded with Erin to change it, as head of security you would have thought she would be able to do something. But no, she had to go ahead.

She had lived with this now for eight months, her stomach extending. Of course her mother was pleased, so was her other parent – or so she was told. What would they know; she was a freak – always secretive. Her friends at school always thought she was weird taking them back to her Grandmother's home. She knew they talked about her behind her back – they said her mother was in an asylum, when she was really stuck in the house with her father – God she didn't even know why. As she got older, she understood why she was not allowed to talk about home and what her father represented was deemed horrendous.

The guilt rippled through her body. An unwanted image invaded her mind of a little girl running through the vines she smiled despite herself playing hide and seek as a tall blonde man was running after her, both of them laughing until he caught her and swinging her up-in the air. My Dad, she thought she loved him, just wished she were more 'normal'. The family secret.

Eva resented that she had been picked for the lottery; she didn't want to be different since she was eighteen, and she wanted to erase her weird childhood into the dustbin. The only person she looked up to was Erin. That was someone to aspire too. Ceres irritated her with her ideals; they were never going to happen. Her mother was always critical, anything she did was not quite good enough. Other mothers were proud of their children getting into the pyramid. Ok she was not a high-ranking member yet – it would come. Now it would not, she was to be a carrier. This was her last day; she didn't want to go into confinement; all those women, talking about babies – Yuk. Grandmama had been nagging about going home – no way.

"How are you feeling?" Hannah asked.

"Not so bad – a lot fatter than you" Eva forced a smile on her face. Hannah didn't understand, how she felt, she had been hoping her name had come up even offered to swap. Rules were rules according to everyone else. Although, Eva resented being different – it didn't occur to her that she also wanted to rebel, when something was not to her liking.

"Are you coming?" Hannah asked, she was worried about her friend. Eva showed no sign of wanting this baby – she had to stop work, there was no way it could be changed. Hannah thought Eva was lucky, being able to take time off. Her own life reminded her of bees, not stopping until you are seventy. Staying at home and still getting your salary for five years seemed a bonus. Hannah who hated her job as much as Eva hated it, but Eva was ambitious; it put her behind in her career path.

"You know I think it would be a good idea for you to go into the institute, staying at home will kill you." Hannah spied a look at her friend. She winced. "At least you will have a back up and support group, other than your Grandmother."

"Hannah how many times do I need to tell you I find those places claustrophobic." She snapped. As they walked away from her desk, Eva didn't even log out; if she had to do this, she was not going to be helpful. Hannah knew not to argue when she was in these moods. Eva had always been moody but recently having a conversation with her was hard work. She drifted off in her own world sometimes for hours.

They walked in silence towards her grandmother's apartment; Eva had stayed with her grandmother since she left home. She rarely spoke of her mother – once she mentioned that she was a monitor. Hannah didn't push the issue she wondered if she looked like Eva? They were the elite; it was never mentioned by Eva again, every time she had asked in the past Eva clamed up or changed the subject entirely.

"Do you want a juice?" Eva asked, more out of courtesy than wanting the company.

"No, I won't, I've got to go back to the department." Hannah didn't want to hurt her feelings.

"I'll see you tomorrow though. It's rest day, so we can go out somewhere nice."

"Yes that would be lovely." Eva said giving her friend a hug.

Eva waved at Hannah as she returned the way they had come. She turned to climb the staircase; it seemed higher than she remembered. As each month went by the stairs were harder to climb – her breathing was shallow as she took a step at a time, the pain in her legs pulsed as the skin stretched tight around her ankles. She felt guilty about Hannah; she didn't mean to take it out on her. She couldn't stand the fact that they were both jealous of each other, it was getting unbearable. She entered the apartment, wishing her Grandmother were there to welcome her. Even if she just gave her a cuddle. Eva collapsed stripping off her top the relief oozed out of every pore. Her cat seized the opportunity for a cuddle, Eva smiled her father had sent it to her as a birthday present two years ago.

Quiet moments were the worst, loneliness over took her; she had no one else to blame but herself. She had ostracised herself from her family, she missed them but she was too proud. Her movements were reported back daily, via her grandmother she could never get away not really. Eva shut her eyes; it had not always been like this. She remembered playing horses with her father, in the orchard or hide and seek, jumping out at her mother, they had found it great fun, everything had changed, once she had started school.

23

Phillip was feeling twice his age, trying to harvest the grapes, he smiled to himself; even his mother was healthier than he was. His left hand automatically returned to the base of his spine, as another shooting pain ran into his legs. The lack of medical treatment was starting to show. He didn't care, he would have been dead long ago - if his mother had not risked everything.

He started to cough, his upper body spasmed, the hacking spewed up more and more mucus. Phillip collapsed onto the harsh dry grass which lay between the vines. He felt weak and pathetic. The basket of grapes he was holding spilled onto the floor, the grapes stained the yellow parched surface red. He had tried hard to hide it from Faith. She would worry and rant about Eva not being there to help; he had heard the same monologue many times previously. Faith never understood their daughter – he did, only too well; she felt as trapped as he did. Faith had after all had an option.

Another coughing spasm overtook his body, the mucus came into his mouth. He spat the yellow slime onto the floor – it eased the pain slightly. Phillip was starting to worry his chest felt tight, he could hardly breathe, and every breath was laboured. He tried to stand pushing himself up with his arms as he did so his chest constricted, cutting off his airways. He fell as the coughing continued his stomach started to wretch, fear coursed through his body. Shaking violently, as he used the last of his energy, the mucus mixed with vomit spread over the ground. Phillip couldn't catch his breath between coughs, more erupted from his insides, this time mixed with blood. He dimly heard a voice as the blackness enveloped him.

"Phillip!" Faith had heard the coughing. This time it was far worse, she knew he had been trying to hide it, he forgot she heard him every night. The purple, black smudges around her eyes were getting significantly prominent daily. Maria had commented in a quiet moment. Faith ran from the cottage.

"Phillip!" She repeated her cry, there was no answer. Luckily, he was not far away, although she was out of breath by the time she had got to him. He lay unconscious where he had fallen – Faith fell to her knees.

"Nooo!" She screamed, checking for a pulse – relief spread through her body, he was still alive.

"Maria" Faith shouted towards the cottage for help. Thank god she was here, Faith was relieved, she would never have lifted him on her own. Checking his airways Faith could see he was breathing, the stench from the vomit made her feel nauseous. Fear seeped into her awareness as she examined the blood.

"Maria" The animal cry came from her – the fear trickled from her, draining any other emotions with it.

Maria came into view.

"What on Earth" she started to say, then saw her prostrate son. "Oh my God!" Maria clamped her now wrinkled hand over her mouth.

"Help me; we need to get him out of this heat." Faith ordered, recovering her composure from the shock, tapping his face with her fingers, she whispered "Phillip, darling wake up, please." Pleading with the unconscious body, her voice sounded odd using unused soft-spoken tones. Maria was surprised she had forgotten the person she used to know, recently the harshness emanated from her – both of them had taken the toll of their shared secret.

Slowly they picked Phillip up under each arm, his

legs leaving a trail in the dusty soil. Every couple of metres they laid him down on the grass as they gasped for breath. Each time checking his breathing - it was faint. Maria and Faith heaved him onto the sofa – Maria collapsed feeling every old bone in her body. Faith started to strip him of the putrid damp clothes. Dousing his body with water, his temperature was extremely high she didn't need to feel his forehead. The heat radiated from him – intent on what she was doing, Faith never noticed Maria speak into her communicator. It didn't matter anymore what Faith thought, she needed Eva here, and it was her father, no matter what had happened between them. Maria felt a part of her was dying; she didn't need to told, all the fight had evaporated within her, from the exertion of pulling Phillip indoors.

"Communicator – contact Erin Holt now – it is urgent." Erin appeared as a holographic image on her wrist.

"What's the problem? This is extremely risky." Erin said disapproving.

"Get Eva – I don't care how, Leah is dying – Faith doesn't know."

"Are you sure?" Erin replied in hushed tones.

"Yes I've seen it in the Institute." Erin disappeared from her wrist, now all she had to do was to keep him alive – her experience of working in the institute for all those years made her realise it was pneumonia, it was rare but a few had developed it, she knew the symptoms – she had no means to stop it.

"I will take over, go and clean yourself up, we could be here a while." Maria instructed Faith.

"It has never been this bad before, he has had a cough for ages; he will be alright won't he?" Faith asked hoping Maria would give her back her hope.

"I'm sorry." Was all Maria said.

"Eva" Erin's image was on the wall. Eva stirred by physically jumping, her cat disgruntled jumped onto the floor.

"Oh" Eva was surprised; she quickly put back on her top, sitting facing towards the screen. "Sorry Erin, I was asleep," Eva couldn't remember dozing, one minute she was thinking, next she was woken up by Erin. Panicking, she didn't know what time it was.

"Are you awake now?" Erin asked gently, she knew why Maria had contacted her she just wished she didn't have to deceive her.

"Yes – I'm fine; someone seems to have removed my body clock. I'm up all night with back pain or cramps, then fall asleep during the day." Eva's hand went automatically to the side of her face. Erin smiled she had watched Eva from being a little girl and saw this same action every time she was worried or tired.

"How was your last day?" Erin tried to keep the conversation light, she needed her on the hover, and soon.

"Fine, the usual – boring." Eva sighed. "I should be grateful; I'm now having a break."

"Talking of having a break, how do you feel about going on a trip for me?" Erin asked silently crossing her fingers behind her back.

"Anywhere nice?" Eva asked her interest sparked.

"Ha, that's a surprise."

"You and Grandmother have not sorted out some plan to get me home again – have you?" Eva said – annoyed they still treated her like a child.

"Ok I will come clean, come over to my office in half an hour – but bring a bag you will need it." Erin's image vanished from the wall.

Eva slammed her fist onto the soft cushion – as always, Erin had the last word. She knew she would go, her curiosity was raised. Irritated Eva pushed her weary body up and went to pack.

Natasha was in an awful mood, she had missed her period again. At her age, it was ridiculous. Disgruntled her mother's health was deteriorating daily. She had been trying to get the medics to let Vanessa have a break with her, in some dark corner of her mind she wanted to show her mother how well she was doing. They said it was dangerous – Natasha didn't see it at all.

"Get me Sabrina," she barked.

"Yes dear?" Sabrina had aged well, her face had been totally reconstructed.

"Get me in the clinic," Natasha said

"Again?" Sabrina said.

"I know – it's irritating, I wouldn't mind if I enjoyed going to the enclosures, it's more of a habit now."

"When do you want to go?" Sabrina asked.

"I can't go in the next week – make it for two weeks hence." Natasha paused "I have some personal things to take care of."

"I will get you booked in." Sabrina stated.

"Maybe, but I don't want to let it down like I was" Natasha regretted saying it as soon as it left her mouth.

"It doesn't always run that way," Sabrina, stated.

"I don't want to risk it." Natasha said.

24

Erin waited outside by a hover. She didn't want to call Eva back hoping she would turn up soon, it was now forty five minutes since she had last spoken to her. Pacing back and forth, she saw Eva's silhouette walking towards her.

"What are you doing? I told you to be here an hour ago." Erin snapped. She already felt annoyed, as she couldn't contact Ceres who was hoping to accompany her. There was no way; Ceres couldn't get the time off at the moment. She had been training a new member of staff for weeks and just couldn't disappear without notice.

"I'm here aren't I" Eva snapped back, "You are lucky I'm here at all." Eva pulled her face as an unruly child would.

"Look, get into the hover and before you go, I'll explain inside. It is risky you going on your own now, but it is necessary" Erin's chest heaved as they climbed into the hovercraft.

Natasha finished work late that evening and had spotted Erin wandering back and forth, alone. It irritated her that she had never been able to catch her – the so perfect head of department. Silently she stood behind the pillar and waited; she saw the two women is get into the hover.

"Eva sit down," Erin ordered, Eva had used the last of her energy getting there; all her irritation seeped from her, along with her fight.

"You are going home – as you thought" Eva raised an eyebrow and tried to push her ungainly body into a standing position.

"Sit down!" Erin barked, stunned, Eva did as she was told to do. "Your father is ill – seriously ill, if you go tonight you may be in time."

"What do you mean in time?" Eva asked simultaneously knowing and dreading the answer.

"I'm not going to spell it out for you; you are a young woman, now is the time to sort out your differences." Erin pointed to the controls, "the coordinates are already in – your mother and your grandmother will both be at the house – just get there soon." Erin stood up to leave. Seeing if Eva had taken in the news or not, she seemed in shock, not a tear fell from her eyes – she hoped she would be fine.

"When I leave press the green button – I want an update when you get there." Kissing her head Erin left the hover. Natasha saw Erin leave and the hovers motors whirred into life, making sure she was unseen from the pathway Natasha watched Erin walk back into the building. Thinking quickly, Natasha ran to one of the tethered hovers and followed the person she recognized as Eva. What relationship she was to Erin she didn't know, but she was about to find out.

The journey went quickly, for Eva as she stared into nothingness for the duration, dreading what she would find when she got there. The island came into view with the light reaching far into the black expanse of water. The hover jerkily landed onto the beach. Automatically stopping, Eva dragged her bag out of the hover and wound her way towards the welcoming light.

"Grandmother?" Eva called through the open door – the light hurt her eyes – blinded instantly as the door opened. The weight of the door pushed Eva backwards, slightly stumbling. It had been seven years since she left this house, her throat constricted as she forced her way into the whiteness inside. Her eyes adjusted to the brightness, viewing her grandmother knelt on the floor. Her mother was nowhere in sight. It was extremely silent except for the rasping breathing from the prostrate body. Wearily Eva placed her bag on the floor before she entered the room before her.

Maria never noticed Eva's arrival, the light touch of Eva's finger on her shoulder was the first indication she was there. She had made it, Maria thought, releasing some of the tension that she had experienced over the last few hours. Maria's shoulders dropped. She physically lost some of the stress that had riddled her body. Eva never said a word, she couldn't. The shock of seeing her father, he was unrecognisable. His features were sunken and grey, the taught skin was barely covering his skull – he looked like a corpse except he was breathing. He didn't look anything like the man he was – his muscular frame was no more. The man in front of her bore no resemblance to her father. A gasp was the only sound Eva emitted, she couldn't help it.

"Do you need a rest?" Eva asked.

"No I'm fine" Maria replied. "Faith has just gone to bed, she needed a rest.

"I'm surprised she stopped talking long enough to look after him" Eva couldn't help it her mouth had turned into a sneer.

"Enough – we all need to sort this out." Maria snapped, Eva felt as if she was a chastised child.

"Will he be alright?" Eva asked.

"No, with my experience, I know when someone is dying. Faith is living in a fool's paradise thinking he will be fine – but he won't."

Natasha followed the tracks, Eva had left her hover for anyone to see. Natasha hid her transport in the undergrowth. She saw the lights in the distance and followed them. Her training was useful; she never made a sound as she came upon the house. The door was still ajar, where Eva had left it when she rushed in earlier. Natasha sunk down out of sight and listened to the conversation inside.

"Do you think mother is going to be okay with me coming?" Eva asked worried when she would have to face her.

"Once she gets over the shock" Maria was secretly worried about her reaction, knowing she had not consulted Faith before contacting Erin. Eva took the damp cloth from Maria, kneeling in front of her father, she was horrified at the way he stared at nothing. Gently she wiped his forehead, the heat emitted through the cold cloth onto her palm.

His breathing was sporadic and slowing, Maria rushed to wake Faith, leaving Eva alone with her father.

"Dad can you hear me?" She whispered in his ear.

"I'm sorry" Eva voice was barely audible, tears flowed over her cheeks she grasped his hand in desperation everything came flooding out.

"It wasn't your fault and it was mine. I always felt the outsider – no one ever told me anything – they still don't." Why was she talking to him this way; he couldn't hear her. She knew damn well her mother would have something to say. Eva needed to tell him before it was too late – she felt it was already. The guilt rose in her from deep inside – all those years missed, he looked old – how. He was only in his forties?

Phillip moved and started to cough, it was hacking. His contorted face and body left Eva paralysed for a moment.

"Dad" she stroked his beaded wet forehead "love

you", his coughing got worse. He looked at his daughter; his eyes still sparkled as if they were sapphires. Love shone from them. He was so grateful for Eva being part of his life, however short, he knew how lucky he had been. A sharp pain shot through his body, shutting his eyes tightly with her face embedded into his brain, he slowly lost consciousness.

"Mum, Grandmama!" She shouted, "Help me." She hoped someone would hear her. Faith and Maria ran to her, she was holding her father, trying to ease his discomfort.

"Get out of the way" Faith shoved Eva away, nearly knocking her over. Faith moved him onto his side so the vomit and the mucus could run freely from his mouth – it was red. Eva felt sick, still on the floor where the fluid had landed she started to back away on all fours. The blood continued to trickle onto the floor.

Faith was covered in Phillip's blood as she held him in position. Not a tear marked her face. Maria had gone to rinse her clothes, Eva felt redundant as normal. The hacking noise reverberated around the room, steadily it eased. Phillip's eyes were still firmly shut, but the pain seeped away from his face, actually making him look younger, as if he was sleeping peacefully. Maria proceeded to wipe up the blood. Not a word was spoken by any of the three women, Maria was intent on her cleaning and Faith was pointedly ignoring Eva – her own daughter, she loved her intently but she would never understand why she had left.

"How is he?" Eva asked to no one in particular, the light was hurting her eyes.

"Not good" Maria replied.

"What would you care" Faith exploded; she couldn't contain herself anymore.

"I do actually, I couldn't stand living here any longer, do you actually know how I felt constantly saying to my friends "Sorry you can't come to my house' I was ostracised, made to feel unclean, sordid even. What did I have to hide? All the time they were right – I couldn't answer back. All that time you were so engrossed in my father you never noticed me. I was a little girl who needed you, I was trapped here, and it didn't matter as long as I kept my mouth shut." Eva flared at her mother "I just couldn't cope; I wanted to be normal – just miss average." Eva collapsed on the chair and wept. Faith wanted to retaliate but Maria put a protective hand on her shoulder. Faith knew what her daughter was feeling, how many times had she wished her life had been different – all she had to do was visit – just once.

Phillip's breathing was getting sporadic, the time lapse between each break grew, ever longer. Eva, Maria and Faith all beside him waiting. The seconds seemed like hours, each breath was agony – all had given up hope. Sometimes his chest rose and fell, the spaces between the breaths was more prolonged. Slowly the women rose to check his pulse, the silence was oppressive. Phillip's body slowly lost the fight, with a last gasp Phillip's life was extinguished.

Eva watched unable to break her vigilance as his body twitched for the last time. She couldn't believe how ironic it was – he looked better dead than when he was still breathing, a flush of colour and peace radiated from him. Faith cried out and the spell was broken, collapsing over him.

"No!" She wailed, Eva ignoring her moved towards him and kissed his cheek, whispering in his ear as he did so.

"Bye Dad, I love you" turning she removed herself away from the scene. Faith never shed a tear, her anger permeated the room. Maria gently kissed her son's forehead, easing Faith away from the body.

194

"He needs to be buried tonight Faith, let's get you changed, we need to give him some dignity." Maria stated, her thoughts were not so pragmatic. *So much has happened to bring us to this, to bury my precious boy,* she thought.

Natasha watched the women from behind a tree, it was a gloomy night but he could see them clearly in the glade, where the body was now buried - the audacity of it all. They had been hiding a man, she knew Erin was involved. She gasped when she realized who it was, the pieces of the jigsaw fell into place – Erin had to give her a promotion now, all these years kept down. That was what they were hiding. Her mother's babbling had been right but she was certified and removed from the community, so that Erin and Maria could hide their past. Seething Natasha ran back to the hovercraft as the women walked up to the house.

She couldn't believe her luck, the hover whirred into life. What if she hadn't left work at that moment, her mother had paid the price, that beautiful woman left to rot in a drug induced haze, Natasha felt sick. If she had not left then, she would still be as ignorant as she had always been. Now it was different, Erin could wait until the morning. Natasha smiled with anticipation.

"Get me the institution and now." Natasha said to her wrist personal computer.

"Can I help?"

"You can pack Vanessa Gresval's things I am coming to collect her now" She stated and then cut off her communication.

Maria, Faith and Eva were tired each engrossed in their own thoughts. Eva's heart was pounding, at last she would know – hadn't her grandmother said so. The pain in her back was getting stronger, it was stupid doing all that heavy work, she needed to know the truth, and it was over whelming. The rain splashed down on their heads, not one of them noticed.

Exhaustion hung like a blanket over the family, all three were distraught with grief but Eva was burning to know.

"So grandmother – what are the family secrets?"

"Yes I will tell you in full gory detail, but bed first it has been a long night – tomorrow you'll know all of them, I promise." Maria stated.

25

The apartment was cold, somehow it didn't matter; she had a secure feeling when she was here in Maria's home. Erin's world had been on a rollercoaster ride over the last twenty-four hours. Eva's cat weaved in and out of her legs – purring. Erin bent down and ruffled his fur behind his ear it was very soothing. A calmness had possessed her psyche. Now she didn't care, her world was about to change with or without her. The silence was interrupted by the cat as she sat waiting for Ceres. She could have gone home but somehow it seemed sterile and it seemed more appropriate to come here. How long had Natasha known? Erin was horrified – Natasha always thought she knew best, Erin couldn't believe it when she waltzed in the office, that morning.

Erin's computer flickered as it switched off. She was reeling after hearing of Phillip's death. Her eyes were red and sore. The news from Maria made her feel sick.

"Erin darling – how are you today?" Natasha sat on an empty chair – uninvited.

"Is there anything I can help you with?" Erin asked, trying to keep her voice calm, the news still fresh in her mind.

"You can actually" Natasha paused for the effect. "Do you remember some time ago you came to one of my parties?"

"Yes – it was unforgettable" Erin answered.

"As you know the star of the show was Phillip" Natasha wanted to see her squirm, her mother had lost everything and Erin was going to pay. Erin remained impassive. She was still numb and didn't care what this women wanted from her now.

"You knew him well didn't you? I remember the conversation we had." Natasha purred

"He died a long time ago, Natasha where is this going?" Ignoring Erin Natasha carried on.

"So we all thought," Natasha paused "his disappearance was slightly unorthodox" Natasha's smile now disappeared. Both women stared at each other, neither acknowledging what the other was saying. The air crackled, Erin thought Natasha was at last showing her true colours. Natasha broke the tension first.

"As I was saying – his disappearance was unorthodox – you were involved – they said at the enclosure it was on your say so when I checked it out, I was never sure of your views. As I said, he was a favourite of mine."

"Natasha" Erin rolled the word off her tongue "you seem to be wasting my time; all of this is old news."

"I thought so too – his daughter does look like him though doesn't she, she has his eyes?" Erin's face was rigid even after all these years; her emotions were well-hidden, deep inside.

"I'm sorry – I thought we had established the fact he had died."

"So we all thought you have kept him hidden well, all this time – Erin." Natasha was not going to let her deny this. "I followed your protégé yesterday – her father died and as I am sure you are aware of – the funeral was very touching." Natasha moved, shifting her position to make herself more comfortable.

"What is it you want?" Erin didn't see the point of any more cat and mouse games. She was terrified; the ramifications for Eva were not worth thinking about. "Don't forget Natasha – your entertainment over the years have not strictly been lawful either."

"Oh – I'm not worried about that, it wouldn't bring

198

political unrest, every person within the pyramid has been to one of my parties. I made sure of that." Natasha laughed, it sounded hollow as the hate had eaten her soul over the years. "I would like a promotion. I like this department, very convenient, let's be honest you haven't got long before you are put out to pasture." Erin felt her world collapse around her. "As I was saying, I think you need a deputy, someone reliable to take over in a year or so. I also think my mother should be remembered in some way, not forgotten – you did ruin her life after all. She was too dangerous to the establishment. The missing link, you may remember her Vanessal Gresval, we both know there are many others. She didn't know that, did she?" Natasha expelled all her built-up emotions at Erin, she had waited many years to get her revenge.

"What if I don't meet your wishes?" Erin asked – already knowing the answer.

"I think, your little secret could become public knowledge – and anything else you are hiding, I'm sure would be of interest." Natasha stood looking down at Erin.

"Quite odd, I thought I would feel elated," Natasha looked at the woman who had ruined her life. "I feel sorry for you, stuck in this office protecting your friends. I never make that mistake, friends can be an inconvenience. I suggest you have this organised by noon tomorrow." As Natasha turned to leave, she again turned to Erin "I hear the Panopticon is particularly uncomfortable in the rainy season." Erin slumped in her chair; she knew Maria, Faith and Eva were safe at the enclosure.

"Communicator - Ceres Zanuti" Erin said.

"Hi, has Maria told you?" the holographic image of Ceres appeared on the desk.

"Yes I am really upset about it – but I need your

attention, it's important" Erin said in a monotone voice.

"Phillip has just died and you've got something more important!" Ceres was horrified. Erin didn't want to drag this out.

"Natasha saw the burial – she's trying to blackmail me."

"I thought we had got rid of that little runt years ago," Ceres exploded, still raw emotionally from the news that Phillip had died.

"No" she said abruptly "she knows – time's run out for all of us – no I'm not reacting like this because of Phillip." Erin knew Ceres would think she was over the top.

"What do you mean?" Ceres asked.

"I need you to contact your friends"

"But Erin – I thought we agreed not to let that information into the public domain" Ceres was worried; she knew Erin would take the fall for this.

"Don't worry just do it – I'll cope" Erin had already made her decision of what she was going to do. "Just contact me at Maria's when it's done. I need to feed the cat."

"Are you letting Maria know?" Ceres asked.

"I don't think I would be able to contact her, she's too far away. The rainy season always plays havoc with communications anyway." Erin smiled her dearest friend would end up a hero after all this, they will be fine.

"I'll speak to you later" Ceres disappeared from Erin's desk.

"Delete all personal files" if Erin knew anything that would incriminate her... steadily she rose grabbed all her belongings and headed out of the office.

"So basically, I found the anomaly, that's where it

started." Maria ended her story. "Too many people were at risk – those that had helped me and of course, we were protecting you as well as your father." Maria turned to see the lightening that flickered across the sky, a minute later the thunder shook the house.

"If that rain pounds our windows much more, we'll all be wet." Faith laughed. Eva was bemused, although she knew her mother near worshipped her father, the odd thing was she didn't recognize her. The pain in her back was getting worse. She had not said anything to her family. Both her grandmother and mother were watching the pyrotechnics outside. She was not going to stop them, saying anything would add to the horrific experience, she had waited too long. Maria and Faith were staring out onto the glade; they were worried that the hole that housed Phillip wasn't deep enough.

"Mother!" Eva's voice trailed away as the pain seared her stomach. She couldn't sit anymore; Eva fell on all fours as the pain encompassed her whole body.

"Oh my God" Faith held her hand over her mouth as Maria ran to Eva's side. "I thought it was due in a month." Faith exclaimed, bringing over a glass of water.

"It's been known for women to start early – you were lucky, you were within the confines of the institute." Maria struggled to give Eva some ease from the stone floor by putting cushions underneath her granddaughter.

Faith was horrified she had never seen this; she had been anesthetized when her daughter was born.

"Can we get her to the mainland?" She asked, feeling stupid and useless.

"We couldn't cross the water in this." Maria pointed to the worsening weather. "She must have brought it on early, digging that hole." Maria wiped the globules of sweat from Eva's head.

"How long - Eva darling – how long have you had this pain?" Maria whispered.

"Half way through the burial" Eva gasped, struggling with the waves of pain that coursed through her body she was being ripped into two.

"Relax – you could be here a while" Faith said – looking at Maria for confirmation, using the blanket that had not so long ago covered Phillip. They covered Eva who lay on her side gripping her stomach. Both Women took turns in cooling her forehead. Both were emotionally drained but found the strength to help Eva, she needed them now.

"Am I dying?" She gasped frightened "I'm not doing this"

"No my love it will soon be over" Maria lied.

Ceres was soaked as the rain lashed over her, it was warm on her skin. She felt in a state of incredulity – now Phillip had died she had thought, it all would be over. She waited at the dock overlooking the crumbling walls. All her life she had used Erin's position to cover indiscretions with the rebels. Most of the staff whom had worked for the pyramid, all of them had learnt the secrets of the enclosures.

A tap was felt on her shoulder, Ceres turned around to see Betty. She had not seen her for a long time, she had grown old – but hadn't she? Only ten years and she could retire.

"How are you?" Betty asked also noting Ceres looked tired.

"I'm fine – things have changed, my informant has given me permission to release the data. Ceres looked at Betty waiting for her assent.

"I'll go now" Betty gave Ceres a hug. "Thank you and take care," Betty turned as Ceres called after her "contact me when all this is done." Betty nodded, with that she disappeared as quickly as she had come. Ceres felt something so momentous should have been harder to achieve. It was always the small things in life that changed everything. Her unease deepened as she spoke into her communicator.

"Communicator – Erin Holt."

"Yes" Erin was relieved to hear from her; even the purring and comfort of stroking the cat was starting to irritate her.

"It is done" was all Ceres said. She walked through the old docklands towards Maria's apartment, she needed to be there for Erin.

Erin smiled, her friends would need her help no more. She tickled the cat's ears as she gently brought the amber bitter tasting liquid to her lips. It tingled and burnt the back of her throat, steadily putting it on the table. She picked up the bottle and poured the capsules onto her hand.

"So small" she whispered, the edges of her mouth twitched at the irony of them. One at a time she alternated between the tablets and the alcohol, until both bottles had been emptied. Feeling her head getting fuzzy, she moved to lie down; the feeling in her fingers touching the cat's fur seemed so acute, almost electric. She closed her eyes waiting for the inevitable, she felt so cold.

Erin was barely aware of the computer flickering into life.

"Emergency Information" the hollow voice echoed around her head, she could no longer move her hand or open her eyes. The words she could hear seemed distant, trying to stay conscious, she listened intently.

It has been confirmed, that the genetic mutation has

been reversed. An unnamed underground organisation have confirmed this and information has been disclosed to us at media central. A biologist named Maria Stevenson was accused of heinous crimes about forty-four years ago. She found the anomaly and a member of the pyramid has kept this information top secret for about fifty years. The woman's name who was the first to be cleared of the mutation was Vanessa Gresval, who now lives with her daughter. We were lucky enough to get an interview with her daughter Natasha, who stated that none of the lower ranking officials knew of this deceit to the nation. A full investigation has been ordered. Natasha herself will be part of the investigation team. All male genders are to be released from the enclosures. The Pyramid headquarters at the conurbation have been bombarded; we have not seen civil unrest such as this since the last of all wars.

Erin smiled as she took her last breath. Her smile etched on her face forever.

"Erin!" Ceres called into the quiet house "Hi have you seen the News Comm?" she rushed in full of excitement, things were going to be alright.

"Erin!" she gently called, expecting her to answer she saw her sleeping on the sofa. She suddenly noticed the empty bottles and ran over to her friend.

"ERIN – Noooo!" Ceres screamed.

Slinking to the floor tears flowed, sobbing, hardly able to catch her breath, the silence was punctuated by the crack of lightening overhead. Ceres didn't know how long she had sat there but the sky was lighting up to a new day. How much more would they have to pay?

Eva rocked backwards and forwards, the light flickered, the electrical storm had affected the communication system. Maria had tried to contact Ceres or Erin for the last five hours. There were no replies, they were on their own.

"Breathe slowly" Maria whispered. An eerie quiet had spread throughout the house. Most of Eva's clothes were littering the stone floor. Eva thought she was going to die, as her pelvic floor muscles told her there was something trying to get out of her. Her stomach muscles were contracting, steadily pushing out the baby – Faith held her daughters hand – soothing her by rubbing her back. Maria laid her hand on her stomach – it contracted.

"Push now" she ordered. An animal scream emitted from Eva. It was drowned out, as the thunder crashed overhead.

"That's it well done" Maria looked, the muscles had relaxed, she could see a blonde lock of hair. The muscles tightened underneath her fingers.

"OK try again." This time the baby fell into Maria's outstretched hands. The pale yellow liquid spread over the floor.

A cry echoed around the room. Eva relaxed.

"She's ok isn't she?" Maria nodded, the baby was beautiful; steadily she cut the cord and gently cleaned it. Faith stood wanting to see her grandchild.

"Can I hold her?" Eva asked. Faith and Maria looked at each other, neither had expected this. Slowly Maria handed the baby to Eva.

"She's beautiful" the proud mother looked down at her new baby covered to keep it warm. Faith gently undid the wrappings to reveal to Eva her son, she didn't care, it didn't matter, it was a boy.

"It's going to be alright – I just know it will" Eva whispered. Maria realized her granddaughter must be in shock, neither of them wanted to say anything. "Phillip and I are going to be fine."